ANNIE'S ATTIC MYSTERIES®

The Deed
in the Attic

K.D. McCrite

AnniesMysteries.com

The Deed in the Attic
Copyright © 2011 DRG.

Library of Congress-in-Publication Data
The Deed in the Attic / by K.D. McCrite
p. cm.
ISBN: 978-1-59635-383-1
I. Title
2011903182

AnniesMysteries.com
800-282-6643
Annie's Attic Mysteries™
Series Creator: Stenhouse & Associates, Ridgefield, Connecticut
Series Editors: Ken and Janice Tate

10 11 12 13 14 | Printed in China | 10 9 8 7 6 5 4 3 2 1

— Dedication —

This book is dedicated to my sister, Betty McCrite Cleland, who gave me the nurturing attention of a mother, the devoted love of a sister, and the laughter and camaraderie of a friend. Bless you, Sister-dear.

— Prologue —

He rearranged their cargo in the car's deep trunk to make room for the last bits and pieces she brought from the house.

"Did you get your fishing gear, honey?" she whispered, handing over a soft, paper-wrapped bundle. "You don't want to leave that behind."

"I have it, sweetheart. Don't you worry."

Even if they ate nothing but fish three times a day, he wanted to be able to feed his wife and himself.

He wedged the package she had given him between a soft-sided suitcase and small box.

"Careful with that," she said, reaching in and moving the parcel a fraction of an inch to the left.

"What about your cross-stitch?" He kept his voice low. They did not want to be seen or overheard. "I know you don't want to forget to take that with us."

She pointed to the bundle they'd just packed in the trunk.

"That's it right there. And I already have my workbasket in the backseat, just in case I want to work on something after the sun comes up. You know how it relaxes me."

He looked at her beloved, familiar face in the darkness of that night. Starlight and silver illumination from a thin slice of moon were all that shone down. The world around the two of them lay heavy and silent with sleep. He had loved this woman for more than forty years. How could it be that, at this time in their lives, things had come to this deplorable state? This was not what he had planned for, not in his worst nightmares.

He bowed his head so she would not see any of his tears reflect a spark of that scant moonlight. He wanted to be strong for her.

"I'm sorry, my dear. I'm so sorry."

She took his hands in hers and gripped them tightly.

"'Entreat me not to leave thee, or to return from following after thee: for whither thou goest, I will go; and where thou lodgest, I will lodge: thy people shall be my people, and thy God my God.' I meant those promises when I spoke them to you before God and witnesses forty-three years ago, and I mean them at this moment."

He gathered his dear wife into his arms and held her tight against him. They clung to each other as fear and commitment sparred for control. This should not be happening to them. He knew it, and yet he could not stop it.

He looked over her head at the sprawling home with its magnificent pillars and lush, manicured gardens. He had built this estate for their family many years ago, with a promise to lay the world at her feet if she would only believe in him. She had given herself to him, her full heart and all her trust, and he had fulfilled that vow with great joy.

That beautiful house, the envy of so many friends and colleagues, had seen them through triumph and celebration, sadness and weeping. And now …

"Get in the car, dearest, before someone wakes up and sees us," he said hoarsely, turning away.

Quietly they got into the car and silently closed the doors. He started the engine, praying no one heard it, and drove out to the highway. Sneaking away like two thieves in the night, they left their much-loved home. Neither spoke again until the rising sun glowed on their faces and beckoned them toward the new horizon.

— 1 —

Annie Dawson gazed out the big front room window and slipped her arms into an old comfy blue sweater she had crocheted years ago when her daughter LeeAnn was little. These days that sweater had lost its beauty and much of its shape, but it was soft and warm, and it held memories of happy days.

Her view of the Atlantic Ocean, with its restless, white-capped waves could be depressing if Annie allowed herself to give way to such feeling. The water looked gray today, as gray and gloomy as the heavy sky above it. This was one of those rainy spring mornings when she would like to curl up in her favorite chair in front of cheerfully crackling logs in the fire-place with a cup of tea or hot chocolate and her yarn. She would contentedly crochet while the radio played soft jazz or maybe some old classic rock music that made her feel good, like she was a girl again, full of hope and promise.

There were times when chilly, drizzly days like this made her ache for the company of her family and friends back home in Texas—and sometimes, she did still think of Texas as "home." If she were in Brookfield right then, she would not be looking out on a cold drizzle. Instead her vista would probably include a sunny front lawn where grass was beginning to green and new buds were shoving their faces into the daylight. But the longer she lived in Stony Point,

Maine, the less lonely she was. Friendships she had developed while here had opened new doors to new experiences. It had taken a little while for Stony Point citizens to warm up to her, but little by little, she had gained their trust and respect. And if she still lived in Brookfield, she would not be in Gram's lovely old home, nor would she be able to see the ocean from almost every window in the house.

No matter where she lived though, in Texas or in Maine, or even in some exotic locale, she always would miss Wayne, the way he smiled, the way his eyes lit up when he played with the grandkids, the sound of his voice when he whispered endearments to her in the night. She yearned to have him beside her again, to feel the strength of his hand as it clasped hers, the warmth of his kiss against her lips. They had looked forward to growing old together. But Wayne was gone, a victim of heart disease, and she had been alone for almost two years now.

Annie loved Grey Gables, the old Victorian-era home that once belonged to Betsy Holden, her grandmother. Wonderful memories of spending her childhood summers here in this house and Stony Point seemed to cling to every archway, every window, even the old wicker furniture on the broad front porch. Though Grey Gables had been rather run down when Annie first arrived, she and Wally Carson, a local handyman, had been able to spruce up its facade with a new paint job and had repaired or replaced the torn, rusty screens. Together they had trimmed back the overgrown landscaping. There was more to do, of course. The shrubs and trees would need to be trimmed in a few weeks. In a house as old and big as Grey Gables, something always needed to be repainted, repaired or replaced. But Annie felt comfortable in Gram's old home, and gratitude filled her as she thought of her blessings. One of those blessings stood at her feet at that moment.

A soft rub against her ankle and a questioning meow signaled that Boots wanted food, or attention, or both. Annie reached down and picked up the furry gray cat. Boots was one more legacy from Gram.

Annie rubbed the sensitive, velvety ears and smiled as Boots closed her eyes and purred. Annie nuzzled the cat's tiny nose with her own.

"You feeling a little blue too, kitty? It's all this rainy weather, I think."

Boots meowed an agreement. The pair stood a little longer, cuddling and purring, enjoying each other's company. After a bit, Annie gently set the cat on the floor.

"You have food in the kitchen, where it belongs," she said. "Run along now."

Boots blinked up at her, mouthed a soundless "mew" as if waiting for Annie to go with her, but after a bit, with tail erect, and on silent white paws, she trotted off sedately down the hallway for the promised snack.

Outside, the chilly early-spring rain fell in a misty, silvery curtain rather than the thick sheets as it had done the day before. Light rain pleased Annie less than bright sunlight would have and for more than one reason. The Hook and Needle Club would get together for its weekly meeting in just a couple of hours. Never, in all the time since Annie had lived in Stony Point, had a Tuesday passed without a meeting. A cold rain certainly was no cause to call it off today. But the thought of driving in heavy rain to the needlecraft store where the club met left Annie less than thrilled. A Stitch in Time was not that far from Grey Gables, so the commute was short and sweet, but still ... .

She glanced at the slim gold watch on her wrist, then down at her clothes. She had never worn tired old slacks and house slippers to a meeting, and she certainly did not intend to start that day. The damp chill of early April in that part of coastal Maine called for warm jeans, a snuggly long-sleeved sweater and sturdy shoes.

By this time of year, in her part of Texas, tender spring flowers would be out of the ground, and the sunny days would be warm enough for shirtsleeves. For just another moment, Annie allowed herself to indulge in the remnants of homesickness, but she knew she would accomplish nothing worthwhile that day if she did not stop this brooding. She squared her shoulders and shooed the melancholy away.

She took a step back to turn from the window, but paused when she spotted a delivery truck lumbering up her driveway. Why would she be receiving a delivery of anything? She cast about in her mind, searching her memory, but she knew full well that she had placed no orders for anything since a few weeks before Christmas.

Curious, Annie stepped outside, away from the warmth of her living room and into the clammy dampness on the front porch. With a creak of brakes and change of gears, the truck came to a noisy stop. While the diesel engine idled, a young, dark-haired driver leaped out onto the wet ground. She watched him as he raised the cargo door, unloaded a huge packing box onto a dolly and then shoved it toward the porch steps. He looked quite grim for such a young man.

"Hello," Annie said cheerfully as he approached.

"Mornin'," he said grudgingly. Muscles in his arms flexed visibly as he backed up the steps, guiding the dolly as if tugging the lead of a stubborn mastiff.

"My, what an enormous box!" she said, quickly dodging to the left so he would not back right into her, which is exactly what it looked like he planned to do. "What in the world is this?"

"Don't know."

She frowned at the huge carton. There was no logo or any printing on it to identify its origins.

"I think you've come to the wrong place," she said. "I haven't ordered anything for several months."

He lowered the front of the dolly and fussed with his computerized ledger without bothering to glance at her once.

"This is Grey Gables?" he asked, punching in numbers.

"Yes, but—"

"You Annie Dawson?"

"Yes, but—"

He handed her the little electronic gadget.

"Sign." He tapped the screen with his fingertip. "Right there." He pulled loose the attached pen and waggled it. "With this."

She took the pen and the ledger from him. Her name looked odd, nothing like her usual smooth penmanship as she wrote it on the small screen. She gave the ledger back to the silent deliveryman, and he trotted down the porch steps, the empty dolly bumping along behind. The scene made her think of a young boy playing with a little red wagon, except that young man obviously was not having fun. Not that Annie could blame him. Unloading and hauling packages in a cold rain certainly held little appeal, especially since it had intensified, losing that dreamy quality from a few minutes earlier. The deliveryman moved faster.

"Wait!" Annie said. "Would you take this into the house for me, please?"

"Sorry," he called over his shoulder. "Against the rules."

"But how am I supposed to move this big thing into my house?"

"Don't know."

"Wait!"

He jumped into the driver's seat, revved the engine, and made considerable noise as he shifted gears; then the truck growled its way back to the road. Annie stared after it, her mouth wagging like a North Atlantic cod.

"I would have helped *you*," she muttered to the now-absent driver.

She huffed a couple of times, her breath enveloping her face in a white mist. After another moment, she dismissed the curt young man from her thoughts and turned her attention to the box that claimed so much space on the front porch.

She squinted at the rain-spattered address label. It was legible, and there was her name and address, plain as day. She looked at the return label. LeeAnn Sorensen.

"My goodness!" she said aloud. What on earth could her daughter have possibly sent that was so big it needed a box this size? It must cost a fortune to send it across the country.

Surely not the twins, she joked to herself. Though the

box was plenty big enough to hold Joanna and John. And maybe LeeAnn too.

"Hmm." She eyed the box, and then eyed her front door. Maybe she could get it inside.

She pushed the box. It wasn't as heavy as she expected, so no daughter and grandchildren had mailed themselves to Stony Point, Maine. But when she tried to pick it up, the size was too awkward for her to handle, let alone lift. What *had* LeeAnn sent to her, anyway? It was not Annie's birthday. Easter had come and gone two weeks earlier. Mother's Day was still several weeks away.

A brief gust of sea-tasting breeze swept across the porch, bringing rain right along with it.

Annie told herself she needed to get that box into the house right away before the rain got worse and soaked the carton and all of its mysterious contents. She propped open the front door, then half-pulled and half-walked the package to the doorway. She grunted. She groaned. She huffed and puffed as the damp cardboard became more slippery than wet soap between her hands.

Finally, sweaty in spite of the chill, breathless and worn out and a little disgusted, Annie plopped down on the living room floor to stare at the box. One corner was inside, the rest of it was out on the porch, and the entire thing was stuck, just like that. She glanced at her watch again. She would either have to get help to maneuver the box the rest of the way into the house, or she would have to miss the Hook and Needle Club meeting. And she refused to miss the meeting. That day they would be discussing ideas for their next group project. As Annie saw it, she really had no choice.

She hauled herself off the floor, went to the telephone and dialed.

Finished with her breakfast and post-breakfast grooming, Boots sought out the company of Annie, sat on the arm of the sofa and watched, apparently waiting for something exciting to break loose from the box. She broke her steady gaze only long enough periodically to deliver a lick or two to her chest.

"Alice," Annie said as soon as her friend next door answered the phone. "I need *help!*" She hung up and returned to struggle with her futile chore.

In less than a minute, Alice MacFarlane's feisty red Mustang roared up the driveway. Alice bailed out almost before the engine died.

Messy auburn hair wet with rain, blue eyes alight with panic, sneakers on the wrong feet, she leaped up the front steps and screeched, "What's wrong? What's happened?"

Then she saw the box wedged in the doorway like some sort of device to protect against home invasion. She looked across the cardboard barrier at her disheveled, disgruntled friend in the living room. The alarmed expression on her face faded quickly. She burst out laughing.

"Annie Dawson!" she hollered, still laughing. "What in the world? I thought something was wrong."

"Something is wrong." Annie pointed at the box in disgust. "I can't move this crazy carton an inch either way."

Alice laughed even harder.

Annie waved one hand impatiently. "I am so glad you're having a good time, but can you pull yourself together now and help me? Please?"

"Well, good morning to you too," Alice said. It looked to Annie as if her friend tried to stifle her laugh but failed the task miserably.

By the time they maneuvered the huge box into the living room, there were bare minutes to spare before the Hook and Needle Club meeting. The two women silently stared at the carton for a full minute, and then Alice turned to Annie.

"Look at us," she said. She ran her gaze along the complete length of her messy friend. "And I'm no better than you."

She thrust out her feet, showcasing the sneakers with toes pointed away from each other. In spite of her momentary annoyance, Annie had to giggle.

"I'm sorry I alarmed you," she said.

Alice kicked off her sneakers and put them to rights.

"Alarmed is the right word. I nearly called 911 before I left the house. I'm glad I didn't."

"Me too! Can you imagine how embarrassing that would be, them showing up because I couldn't get a box through a doorway."

Alice shook her head, and then pinned her gaze on the carton.

"Okay, girlfriend. The question of the day: What's in the box?"

Annie shook her head.

"I have not the least little clue. It's something LeeAnn sent." She glanced at her watch. "Guess I'll open it when I get back home."

Alice squawked.

"You will do no such thing! You think I can sit quietly and do cross-stitch for an hour or two when I'm dying of curiosity?

Open it, Annie." She grinned and added, "Please?"

Annie hesitated, but only for a moment. Whether or not she showed it, she was more curious than Alice.

"I'll just go get something to cut through this strapping tape."

She rummaged around in her "everything" drawer in the kitchen, pushing aside a set of keys, three blue pens, a couple of screwdrivers, a roll of tape and half a package of gum before she finally laid her hands on the sharp utility knife she was searching for. Alice clapped her hands when Annie returned to the living room, brandishing the knife.

"It's just like Christmas," Alice sang out.

"Isn't it?" They giggled like two little girls.

Annie thrust the tip of the knife into the corded tape and ran it slowly, gently along the top of one side of the box. Alice watched, fidgeting.

"Will you hurry? What are you doing?" she finally asked, impatience coloring her tone. "At this rate we will be here all day." She bent to examine the tape, then shook her head sadly. "Look at that, Annie. You didn't even cut it all the way through."

"Well, I don't want to damage whatever's inside. What if it's full of balloons, or something?"

"*Balloons?* Oh, Annie!"

"Well, you know what I mean. The box might contain something delicate or breakable. I don't want to nick anything."

"I'm sure your daughter packed it carefully. Go for it!"

Annie hesitated just a moment longer. Finally, she forced herself to banish the image of hideous knife marks gouged into the contents, whatever they were.

"Well, then," she said, and pulled the knife through the tape with considerable less delicacy the second time. She guided the blade around the sealed path until all four box flaps were free to be pulled back.

"Now, my friend," she intoned as dramatically as a Shakespearean actor, "we shall see what we shall see!"

Alice leaned forward, smiling, bright eyes sparkling with eagerness and curiosity.

Annie pushed back the flaps. She gasped and took a half a step back when she saw the gift.

"Oh, my goodness! Alice, look. Would you look at that!"

Both women stared wide-eyed at skein after skein of yarn that filled the box almost to overflowing. Annie thrust her hands into the contents with the eagerness of a little kid on Christmas morning, and pulled out armfuls of soft baby yarns in every pastel shade. She lifted out dark durable wools, bright practical cottons and easy-to-use blends variegated in so many shades it staggered her mind.

"Look!" she whispered again, as if afraid Santa Claus would overhear and take the gift back up the chimney. "Oh, Alice, look at this!"

"I'm looking, I'm looking! I have never seen so much yarn in one place in my whole life. Except at A Stitch in Time, of course."

As the women continued to take out the yarn, they discovered at least twenty balls of crochet thread, some of it sturdy as twine and some of it felt as delicate as a spider's web.

"My goodness, Annie. What a treasure trove!"

"Oh, isn't it?"

Halfway immersed in the box, Annie found a second package.

"There's something else!" she shouted as she came up for air.

Alice laughed. "This obviously is the gift that keeps on giving."

"It surely seems that way, doesn't it? Now, what's in here?"

She yanked the brown wrapping off the second package and found it contained at least a dozen crochet pattern books. Accompanying the books was a sealed envelope with the word "Mom" written in large letters across the front.

Annie thrust the books into Alice's hands, grabbed up the letter eagerly and tore open the flap. She silently read the brief note.

"Well? That's a letter from LeeAnn, isn't it?" Alice asked. "What's it say?"

Annie smiled and read aloud. "Dear Mom, Things are going well here, hectic as usual. The twins put all their red and brown crayons in the toaster oven. Don't ask me why. What a mess, though!

"Herb is getting over a nasty cold. He actually missed a day of work last week, but he's feeling much better now. Hope you continue to avoid catching any 'bugs' this year. I'd hate to think of you up there, all by yourself, and sick with a cold."

Annie paused reading long enough to chuckle and say to Alice, "Can you just imagine how much chicken soup the Hook and Needle women would provide if I were to become ill?"

Alice laughed with her. "Gallons!" she said.

Annie continued to read. "Yarns Galore here in Dallas had a going out-of-business sale this week. I couldn't resist buying some crochet goods for you. Please think of me as you use this yarn. Hope you enjoy it! I miss you so much and love you even more! Hugs and kisses from J & J. Love, LeeAnn."

With her eyes swimming, Annie looked up and smiled at Alice.

"Of course I'll think of her when I use this yarn. I think of her, every day. I think of them all every day."

"Oh, Annie," Alice said softly. "I know you miss them."

The smile Alice gave her brought more tears to Annie's eyes, but she refused to give in to any melancholy, especially when she would be meeting with her friends very soon. She flicked the tears away with her fingertips and took a deep breath.

"You know what?" she said, glancing at her watch. "We're going to be late for the meeting, and we both look like we've been working in a barn."

Alice laughed and headed for the door. "As long as we don't *smell* like we've been working in a barn, I'm happy! And you know, I seem to be late more often than not these days," she said as she went outside. "See you soon, Annie."

After Alice left, Annie realized she had not even thanked her dear childhood friend for helping.

2

"What happened to you?" Peggy Carson called out the minute Annie entered the comforting, dry warmth of A Stitch in Time.

Annie was breathless, wet and cold. She held her tote bag clutched close to her chest to keep her crochet project dry. She resisted the urge to shake all over like a wet dog.

Annie felt a little disconnected from the present moment. She had taken a few minutes before she left Grey Gables to call LeeAnn, and now their conversation lingered in her mind, soft and bittersweet.

"Honey, this box of yarn you sent is the most generous and thoughtful gift anyone could have given me," she had said almost as soon as LeeAnn answered the phone.

"I'm so glad you like it, Mom."

Annie could almost see the smile on her daughter's face.

"Mom?"

Annie heard wistfulness replace the smile a moment later.

"Yes, honey? What is it?"

"I guess this will sound a little silly, but sometimes, especially lately it seems, right before I go to sleep at night, I have this memory. It is so crystal clear that it's like it is really happening."

"It must be a very special memory, then. What is it?"

"Well, it's something I remember from when I was a little

girl. It's bedtime, and I'm in my pajamas, and I go into the room to give you a good-night kiss. I see you sitting in your favorite chair, that soft rose-pink one that used to belong to Grandma. Daddy is usually in the recliner with his feet up, and he's reading or dozing. A cup of tea sits on the table next to you, and your head is bent over hook and yarn. In my memory, there is always music playing, and you always have a little smile on your face as if you're just so happy."

Tears stung Annie's eyes. She knew that memory; she thought of it often as LeeAnn grew up and no longer kissed her good night every night. This memory rubbed a wound in her heart. She missed her family so much!

"That happened nearly every night, honey," she said with forced light-heartedness, "until you got too old for such mush."

LeeAnn laughed. "Mush. I forgot that word."

"LeeAnn," Annie said, trying to banish the blue mood that seemed to be growing, "do you remember when you would read the crochet pattern directions to me phonetically. *Ch 1, sk next ch-3 sp.* All those little bits of words spurting like drops of water. It was so funny. We would laugh so hard that you would finally have to stop reading just so you could breathe."

"I remember! I loved doing that."

They laughed together again for a moment, and then the laughter faded.

"Mom?" Annie heard the pensiveness in her daughter's voice again. "I'm not trying to be all somber and mopey-sounding, but I've been wondering ... with your new life and all your new friends, do you ... well, I mean, you *do* still miss us? Don't you?"

LeeAnn's need for reassurance played Annie's heart-strings, striking twin chords of sympathy and full under-standing.

"Oh, honey, *yes!*" she rushed to assure the younger wom-an. "More than you know. How could I not? You and Herb, and the twins ... you are my dear family. Listen to me. This is important: I will *never* make so many friends or have so much to do that I will stop missing y'all every day. *Never!*"

LeeAnn's chuckle was a little watery.

"I guess I sound like a spoiled brat, don't I?" she asked.

"No! Not at all."

"I just wanted to hear you tell me again." Annie heard her inhale deeply and blow out the breath. "Mom, I just wish we had spent more time together while you were still living down here."

Annie wished that too. In fact, she had wished it often even while she still lived near LeeAnn. But her daughter had her own busy life, full of babies and friends and work. More often than not, Annie had felt she was unnecessary, perhaps even somewhat underfoot at times. Too bad it had taken Annie's absence to prove LeeAnn's devotion.

"Well, don't think about that, honey. Just be sure you spend lots of time with your own kids and with Herb. Don't you ever doubt, not even for a fraction of a minute, that your mama misses you terribly."

"Okay, Mom. I'll try. And don't *you* forget that you're coming down for a visit in the fall. Right?"

"Right. If all goes according to plan."

"Then we'll just have to be patient until we see each other again, won't we?"

"Yes," Annie sighed. "We surely will."

And she would, tough as it was to wait. LeeAnn's words had pricked an old scar in the melancholy mood Annie had battled for the last several days. She was determined not to fall prey to more gloomy meanderings. For now, it was enough that she had her projects, and she had her friends, and right then, those friends were sitting a few feet away, looking at her, waiting for Annie to greet them.

Giving a smile to the group in general, she set the tote on the floor next to her, shed her raincoat and hung it on the coatrack that Mary Beth Brock, the shop's owner, had provided for the members of the club. She fluffed her chin-length blond hair with her fingers, glanced down at her burgundy blouse to make sure she was buttoned and straight, and then looked around the cozy group and retrieved the tote.

"Good morning, all," she said as she settled into her chair. From the bag, she pulled out her current work-in-progress, an ecru pineapple table runner. It would match the two place mats she had already completed.

She had been so used to working with worsted yarn that when she began this project, the delicate cotton thread felt strange and thin in her fingers. At first she had taken out as many stitches as she made until she finally grew accustomed to the small hook and slender thread. Lately, though, as she worked, the silver hook flew from stitch to stitch as fast as the larger ones did when she crocheted afghans and throws.

The door opened, letting in damp air and the constant sound of rain as it battered the sidewalk and street. Alice burst into the shop, gave everyone a distracted glance and let the door close behind her.

"Does anyone know where the phrase 'raining cats and dogs' comes from?" she asked the group. She slicked drops from her denim jacket and jeans and slid her booted feet across the small mat at the entryway.

The women exchanged mystified looks, and in nearly perfect unison, they said, "No."

"I've never even thought about it," Peggy added. Slightly chubby, with short dark hair, Peggy gave the world the impression of fun and enthusiasm. Her pink and white uniform offered a spot of cheerful color on such a rainy day. Peggy obviously would be working at The Cup & Saucer later that afternoon. "I take it you know the answer, Alice?"

"As I was driving here, the fellow on the radio said he had looked it up on the Internet and found that, in all likelihood, it came from seventeenth century England when a lot of rain would flush out debris and among it would be dead dogs and cats—and other things too disgusting to mention—that would go floating by."

"Oh, Alice, that is truly revolting!" dark-haired Kate Stevens said, looking up from the counter where she was straightening a rack of novelty buttons. Everyone agreed with her.

"Well," Alice sniffed as she settled into her chair, "I just wanted all of you to know that it is *not* raining cats and dogs ... yet." She glanced around. "Where's Gwendolyn?"

The words were barely out of her mouth when the door opened again. Gwendolyn Palmer, every inch Stony Point's leader in fashion and style, greeted the others.

"So sorry I'm late. The rain is just terrible!" She removed a tailored sea-green raincoat and hung it on the rack with everyone else's jackets or coats. A matching, wide-brimmed hat sat saucily atop her head. When she took it off, her short blond hair looked as chic as ever. One thing about Gwendolyn, she always looked perfectly put together every time Annie had seen her.

Gwen settled down and plucked up her knitting from a forest green tote.

"My goodness," she said, looking at the half-finished chocolate brown sweater she held up for display. "Here it is April already, and I had planned to have this done in February. Well, John has waited all this time, so I guess he can wait a little longer and wear it next winter."

The group shared a chuckle, but they realized a woman as busy as Gwen did not always sit down and knit. She always seemed to be busy in civic affairs around Stony Point. Annie liked the woman and was glad Gwen rarely missed the weekly Hook and Needle Club meetings.

"I hope to have this wall hanging finished by the end of the month," Peggy said. She gazed down at the quilting project on her lap. The pattern was a lush green palm leaf on a pale blue background—simple but refined. Her tiny neat stitches added to the overall elegance of the piece, and anyone who looked at it could see the love Peggy had for her work.

From her gray-and-red plaid tote, Alice lifted out the cross-stitch covering she was making for a miniature picture frame. It was to be a gift for a cousin in New Hampshire who was expecting a baby at the end of May. The tiny yellow and white design seemed to herald springtime and new life.

"I just love that," Annie sighed, looking at Alice's neat handiwork. "It's like you're holding a bit of sunshine in your hands."

"Thanks, Annie," Alice said, smiling. "And your project is terrific! I love it more every time I see it. I can't wait to see it spread out on your dining table some evening, with Betsy's Aster Blue china, and her crystal goblets, with candlelight flickering. ... "

Annie smiled and said nothing. The notion was too romantic for her palate right then. Somehow romance just was not on her list of priorities since Wayne passed away.

My dear husband! Now he was a romantic guy, she thought silently, *full of tender surprises*.

Then she realized she was doing it again, allowing herself to fall into the glum clutches of gray, rainy days that looked as if they would never end.

With determination, Annie shoved aside sadness and concentrated on the delicate lacy work in her hands. She planned to give the runner and place mats to Alice for her birthday a few weeks from now.

"Ladies, may I have your attention so we can discuss our next group project?" Mary Beth said, standing in the center where they could all see her.

In her blue slacks and matching sweater, Mary Beth's stocky build and her kind but firm voice gave the woman an air of comfortable authority, like a well-liked teacher. The silvery threads of gray running through her dark hair caught the light from the overhead fixtures as she looked at the group.

"The other day I was visiting with one of the women who

works at the Seaside Hills Assisted Living," she said, "and she told me she had overheard a few of the resident ladies talking. She said the women were saying how much they wished they had footwear that was softer than their usual house slippers but warmer than the socks that are available in stores. Well, that got me to thinking, and I wondered why couldn't we, the Hook and Needle Club, make slippers for those residents?"

She turned first to curly-haired Peggy.

"You could make quilted ones, couldn't you, Peggy, and Alice could add cross-stitch along the sides or top. And Stella, I'm sure you can knit slippers, right? Gwen, you just said you were not going to force John to wear that sweater until autumn." Everyone laughed, and she added, "I'm sure Annie and Kate can whip out a few pairs of slippers with their crochet hooks."

"That sounds like a great idea!" Kate said, fairly bouncing with enthusiasm. "I have a good pattern for some really cute slippers. It's pretty simple so it won't take very long to crochet several pairs."

Stella Brickson, the oldest member of the group, put her knitting needles in her lap and stared above the heads of the women at nothing.

"I haven't made slippers in years," she said slowly, thoughtfully. "I'm not sure I can remember how."

"Of course you can!" Peggy said. "It'll be like riding a bicycle."

Stella gave her a narrow look, and then she picked up her needles again.

"I'm not getting on a bicycle for anyone!" she declared.

Everyone laughed at that, not only because the prim and proper Stella rarely joked, but also because the vision of the octogenarian on a bicycle seemed so outrageous. After a moment, she laughed with them.

"So we're all agreed?" Mary Beth asked, meeting the eyes of each woman.

"Agreed!" they replied, almost in unison.

For only a moment there was a small silence in the store, broken by the sound of rain outside, the rhythmic click of knitting needles, and the soft whisper of thread moving over hooks or through fabric.

Like an antsy toddler, Alice twitched in her seat several times. She cleared her throat once, twice, and then again. Finally she said, "Well, Annie?"

Annie looked up from her crochet hook. "'Well, what?"

Alice twisted her mouth. "You know what. Are you going to tell them?"

She said this loud enough that every crafter stopped work, and every pair of eyes rested with bald curiosity on Annie. Alice was right. Annie knew exactly what she was referring to, and she wanted to share the news of LeeAnn's gift—she really did. But during the entire time she had showered and changed clothes before coming to the meeting, she had thought of Mary Beth Brock, and Mary Beth's store. Her gaze went to the woman now. Mary Beth was smiling, waiting expectantly for whatever good thing Annie would tell them.

The problem was—and she was surprised that Alice did not realize this—Annie bought all her crochet yarns and threads from Mary Beth. She never even shopped for supplies when she went to Portland or any neighboring town. Now she would not need to purchase anything for a long time. How would Mary Beth feel about losing sales? Would she understand, or would she feel betrayed? Annie had seen firsthand how business could get in the way of friendship. Not everyone had the knack for successfully separating or consolidating the two. She did not want to lose Mary Beth's friendship.

Of course, Annie could continue to buy yarns and add to her stockpile. Mary Beth need never know that in Annie's home a huge supply waited to be worked up into projects. She could simply—

"Earth to Annie!" Peggy called.

Annie blinked, her train of thought completely derailed and brought back into the here and now.

"Are you going to tell us this mysterious tidbit, or shall we let Alice?" Stella said, eyebrows raised. "It's perfectly clear she's bursting with it."

Annie stared at the eager faces turned to her. Oh, dear. Would they still be smiling like that after they knew?

"LeeAnn sent her a great big humongous present!" Alice blurted before Annie could take a good, deep breath.

The women twittered like a flock of wrens.

"Do tell," Gwen prodded.

"For heaven's sake, yes. Why are you dragging it out like this?" Stella pinched her lips in disapproval, but she could not disguise the interest shining behind her eyeglasses.

"Well, actually—," Annie began. She shot at look at the store manager, "and I am so sorry, Mary Beth—but you see, LeeAnn sent me this large box— humongous, as Alice said—of ... of *goods* from a store in Dallas."

Mary Beth raised her eyebrows.

"Goods?" she echoed.

"What kind of 'goods'?" Kate asked. "Like household items or clothes or what?"

"Um. No."

Annie fiddled with a couple of stitches, fumbled and had to unravel them. *Just get it over with*, she thought.

She took a deep breath and looked Mary Beth in the eyes.

"Well ... it's yarn," she finally blurted. "Lots and lots of yarn. And tons of crochet thread. And a bunch of pattern books. I am so sorry."

While all the other women made appropriate noises of good-natured envy and happiness, Mary Beth stared at her.

"You're sorry? Why on earth are you apologizing to me? That is a wonderful gift to receive at any time, and any crafter would be ecstatic to get it!"

"Well, because ... you know."

"No, I don't know," Mary Beth said with a puzzled frown creasing her brow, "and I don't understand."

"Because, well, because I won't need to ... ." Annie took a deep breath and then exclaimed, "I'll still buy yarn from you!"

Mary Beth blinked, but her confusion obviously remained.

"Annie, why would you do that?" she asked. "Sure, I like having your business and I welcome it anytime you want to buy anything from the store, but I'll survive just fine, even if you don't buy yarn from me for a few weeks."

"But, Mary Beth, you don't understand. It won't be just a few weeks. It likely will be months. Maybe even a year or two."

"So? Annie, I'll still survive." The woman gave Annie a warm smile. "We are friends. And even if you never bought another inch of yarn from me, that would not change. So you enjoy your gift from LeeAnn with a clear conscious. Okay?"

Annie's relief rushed through her. She gave Mary Beth a grateful smile.

"Yes. Okay. Thank you, Mary Beth. That's a load off my mind."

"What a terrible fuss over nothing," Stella muttered, shaking her head. "You'll get along a lot better in Stony Point, Annie, if you don't turn into a drama queen." She glanced around at the others. "Isn't that what they call it these days? 'Drama queen'?"

Kate piped up. "Annie is *not* a drama queen. She's just tenderhearted, and she didn't want to hurt a friend."

"And she didn't hurt me—not in the least," Mary Beth said stoutly. The phone on the other side of the counter rang, and she went to answer it.

"Oh, you ladies should have seen the two of us get that box into Annie's house!" Alice said, laughing. "It was wild!"

She related the events of the morning, but added such embellishments, complete with broad gestures and wild-eyed expressions that she had most of the women laughing so hard they had to lay aside their work to wipe tears from their eyes.

"But getting that shipment of yarn into the house was the tip of the iceberg, I'm afraid," Annie said when Alice ceased her storytelling and everyone had quieted. "The problem now is that I have a gigantic cardboard box in the middle of my living room and more yarn than I've ever seen at one time. And I have no idea where to keep it."

"What are you worried about?" Peggy said, scoffing. "You have that big attic, don't you?"

"Peggy!" Annie chuckled and shook her head. "Have you ever seen Gram's attic?"

"I have!" Alice said, raising her hand as if she were in a schoolroom.

"Me too," added Gwen. "I saw it a few years ago when Betsy took me up there to find vintage clothes for the high school 1920s pageant. That attic was stuffed to the rafters."

"I have cleared out a lot, believe it or not," Annie said, "but I'll tell you something. It is still stuffed to the rafters. Gram had an efficient way of packing things away. I think her motto must have been, 'let no space go unused.'"

~ 3 ~

"This attic is darker than the inside of a cow." Annie's voice sounded odd in the quietness of the attic as the silly old country saying came echoing back from somewhere in her Texas past. If the inside of a cow was as dark as the attic on a rainy afternoon, it was pretty dark.

She stood, hands on hips, squinting into the dusty, dim interior. The place never was full of light, even on a sunny, cloudless day. With the spring rain hanging on as if it was afraid to move from Stony Point, the attic was even more shadowy.

"Spooky," she murmured.

"What is?"

The voice behind Annie made her heart leap in her chest. She whirled, dizzy with fright.

"Alice!" She clasped her fist to her heart, trying to slow its wild hammering. "You scared me out of a year's growth. I may never recover."

"I knocked," Alice told her. "Many times. I called your name. Many times. Anyway, at our age how much growth would we really lose in a year?" She peered around, her gaze probing the far corners. "It *is* spooky in here."

"No, it isn't. Not really. It's just … dark."

"Um hmm. Well, excuse me, Annie Dawson, but I just heard *you* say 'spooky.' What are you looking for this time? A place to hoard your stash of yarn?"

"In a manner of speaking. Actually, I need something better than that cardboard box LeeAnn sent it in."

"I see. Every time I see this attic, I'm amazed by how many things it holds. My goodness! You ought to find something up here. What a collection!"

Annie nodded and looked around, scouring the area with her own gaze.

"You are one hundred percent right, m'dear. It is a grand collection, isn't it? And a month or so ago, I thought I saw ... yes! There it is. Right over there."

She picked her way past hat boxes and baskets, two old baby dolls and a tricycle. She moved aside a Victorian floor lamp with a beaded-fringe shade. Alice followed.

"Right here!" Annie said, stopping. "This is just the thing."

Alice edged around the small space to look. "A cedar chest."

"A *big* cedar chest no less! And the cedar lining will protect the fibers of the yarn."

"Aren't you the clever one?" Alice grinned.

"I've always thought so, yes."

"And so modest too." Alice feigned wide-eyed admiration.

"Of course. That's one of my strongest qualities."

The two friends shared a giggle, and then turned their attention to the chest and studied it for a minute.

"But do you think it's big enough?" Alice asked. "I mean ... that's a lot of yarn you have down there in the living room."

"Yes, it is." Annie chewed her lower lip, staring at the dusty lid. "Well, I'll just have to see what I can do. In the meantime ... ."

She bent to grasp the wooden handle on one end and lifted.

"Umph!" she gasped, tumbling forward slightly. "I'll throw my back out of place trying to hoist that thing."

"Yeah, solid-wood chests seem to have a little weight to them," Alice said drily.

"Ha, ha. Help me move it, will you, please?"

Alice made a show of flexing her arms like a wrestler, and then she bent to grasp the handle on the other side. With some grunting and grimacing, the duo was able to wag the trunk along the cluttered pathway and out the attic door. The attic staircase, steep and narrow, presented a treacherous descent. Taking one step at a time, with Annie going backward, they hauled the chest down—thump, pause, thump, pause—until they reached the landing and the broader staircase leading down to the main floor.

For a moment, the women paused, stretched out the kinks from their backs, arms and shoulders, took a couple of deep breaths, and then returned to their task. Slowly, with Alice taking the steps backward this time, and with much pushing and tugging, they lugged the heavy cedar chest down the second flight of stairs and into the living room.

Boots, who had been napping on a windowsill, woke up, saw them and took flight to hide behind a burgundy chenille wing chair. She peered out at them with suspicion.

"Well, that was a whole lot of fun, wasn't it?" Annie said as they collapsed on the floor. She had already unpacked and examined every skein and ball, and she had sorted them by color and by blend. The worsted yarns were piled in organized stacks on the sofa, solid colors then variegated ones.

Solid crochet threads filled the wing chair and the variegated threads were in the armchair. Chunky yarns took up the second armchair.

Alice let her gaze rove around the room, and then she gave Annie a sour look.

"Are you kidding me? First we move that oversized, wet box, and then that heavy cedar chest. What's next on your list? Hoist that piano over there up the stairs to your bedroom?"

Annie glanced at the upright on the far wall, and then laughed at her friend.

"I'm sorry. But I'm so glad you were here to help me both times. Would you like some coffee?"

"Coffee would be great. Maybe it will strengthen my blood. But, please, can we just sit here a few minutes and catch our breath first?"

Annie agreed, and they sprawled out where they were on the floor, resting on their elbows, legs stretched out. Silence lay comfortably between them for a little while.

"Say," Alice said lazily, lolling her head Annie's direction, "that cedar chest is empty, isn't it? Don't tell me we dragged down a chest full of stuff."

"Of course, I—" She froze in place, staring at Alice. "Uh oh," she said slowly.

In all the emotional ups and downs of that day, something as mundane and logical as checking to see if any contents filled the cedar chest before they hauled it down two flights of stairs had not even occurred to her.

"Uh oh?" Alice repeated, pinning her with a glare so steely that Annie shrank a little inside herself.

"Oh," she said, in a small voice. "Everything in Gram's

attic is full of stuff, so I guess it probably is."

Alice closed her eyes. Tight. "Oh, Annie."

Annie bit her lower lip. "I'm sorry."

Alice sighed deeply and opened her eyes.

"If you weren't one of my oldest and bestest friends, Annie Dawson, I think I would absolutely clobber you. I'm no spring chicken, you know!"

They stared at each other for a bit, and then Alice's expression changed. Annie felt her own face relax. A moment later they both collapsed into giggles.

"Well, let's not just sit here," Annie said when they sobered. "Let's open this chest and see what we carted down."

They scooted up closer to the dusty trunk. Annie looked at the lid and found the clasp.

"I hope it isn't locked," Alice said as Annie pushed a little metal button to release the catch. "I'm trying to put aside my past as a lock picker."

Annie gave her a sideways look.

"Luckily for all of us Stony Point citizens who tremble in fear at your criminal prowess, this particular chest doesn't seem to be locked."

"Just kidding," her friend said, pulling a face. "I've never picked a lock in my life."

"We can all sleep safely in our beds at night," Annie said with an exaggerated sigh of relief.

Alice rolled her eyes, and Annie laughed.

"Well, let's see what's in this baby."

Annie heaved open the heavy lid. The hinges cried out in rusty protest.

"Yow. Sounds like I need to get a can of lubricating oil."

Inside the trunk, the red cedar wood with its thin veins of white and small, dark knots, offered up woody fragrance as aromatic as if it had been freshly cut.

Alice breathed deeply. "I love the scent of cedar."

"So do I," Annie said, running her fingertips across the smooth wood inside the lid. "Wayne and I had cedar-lined closets back home. They were so nice."

Alice studied her a moment.

"You're really feeling down, aren't you, girlfriend? I've noticed it for the last couple of days, and you haven't been yourself."

"It's just the rain," Annie said briskly, dismissing her friend's concern. She did not want to burden Alice with a melancholy mood that would fade sooner or later. "Now, let's see what we have."

She looked at the top layer.

"Old papers and old clothes," she said, lifting it out. "I didn't expect anything else." She extracted more of the same and then sat back on the heels of her hands, tipping her head sideways and added, "Now where will I put all this stuff? I was hoping to store yarn, not unearth more things to put away."

"I know," Alice said with sympathy. "Would you like me to help you sort through it?"

Annie knew Alice had other and better things to do than paw through a trunk of old stuff. Her offer touched Annie, reminding her what a good friend Alice was.

"Don't you have a Divine Décor party?" she asked.

Alice made her living by holding home parties where she sold Divine Décor to embellish the home, and lovely

Princessa Jewelry to embellish the home owner. Alice loved to model the jewelry on every occasion, and her bubbly personality along with her friendly nature made her a perfect representative for both lines of products.

Alice waved one hand dismissively, and then she reached into the trunk again. She removed a stack of faded scarves.

"No parties until tomorrow. Oh, Annie, look! These are lovely. Pure silk, I'm sure." She stroked her fingers along the soft fabric of the top scarf. The silver rings on her fingers shone like ice against the dark purple.

"Why don't you take them?" Annie said.

"But they're so beautiful, Annie. You should keep them, and wear them."

"I want you to have them, Alice. Please, take them all. Look how they set off your jewelry. Use them in your parties for display."

Alice caressed the scarves. "You're sure?"

"One hundred percent."

"Well, then. Thanks! And what a great idea to use them with the jewelry. You're terrific, Annie."

"I know."

"Oh, please. Let's not start that again!"

They laughed, and Alice leaned forward to peer into the trunk once more.

"What else is in here, I wonder?" she murmured.

She pulled out an old leather-bound Bible, obviously much loved and well-used, but with no marks or inscription to offer an owner's name. She lifted two sets of tarnished old keys and frowned at them.

"What you suppose these open?" she asked, jiggling them.

Annie took the long, thin keys, and gave them a cursory examination.

"Who knows? But they don't make 'em like this anymore."

She set them down on the floor beside her.

Next came a box of embroidered lace handkerchiefs, and a falling-apart cookbook.

"You know," Annie mused, "I guess I ought to be tired of going through all these old things I find in the attic, but I'm not. I love finding the treasures."

"Me too," Alice said. "You know how close Betsy and I were, especially in those months right after John and I divorced. It didn't matter that we were decades apart in age. We were still good friends. Going through these things makes me feel closer to her somehow. Does that make sense?"

"Makes perfect sense to me," Annie replied, "because I feel the same way."

They shared a smile, and then Annie delved into the chest again.

She removed a red-and-white gingham apron, cross-stitched with a primitive barnyard scene. The work was simple and neatly done, but obviously not the style or advanced skill level of Betsy Holden's works. Besides, Gram's work was art, not wearable clothing.

She picked up a thick packet of paper that had been folded in thirds, encased in a thick yellow cover and fastened with an attached band.

"This looks official," Annie said.

"It does," Alice agreed, watching with interest as Annie unfastened the band.

She unfolded the papers and looked at the top

document. "Abstract of Title."

"Must be the deed to this place," Alice said. "But I wonder why it was in the attic? Shouldn't property deeds be kept in a security box at the bank?"

"The deed to Grey Gables is in a box at the bank," Annie told her.

Alice looked confused. "But why would there be two?"

Annie glanced through a couple of pages, frowning.

"This is not the deed for Grey Gables. It gives a different property location and it mentions 'Fairview.'"

"Fairview!" Alice squawked. "Are you kidding?" She scooted over next to Annie on the floor and looked at the deed.

"What about it? Where is it? What is it?"

"Fairview. Oh, my goodness, Annie. It's an awful old place on Doss Road north of town. In fact, everyone calls it 'Foulview.'" She pointed to a name on the deed. "I wonder who Joseph and Alta Harper are?"

Annie shook her head. "I don't know, but ..." she flipped the page over "... Gram got the place from them. There's her name, and all the legalese that states her claim to the place. In fact, the way this reads, it looks like they just gave it to her."

"Yikes," Alice said softly, after a bit.

Annie slid a sideways glance at her. "It really is as bad as all that?"

"Worse."

Annie stared at the deed without seeing it for a moment. Why had Gram never mentioned owning any property but Grey Gables? Was this Fairview place really as awful as

Alice indicated? Surely Betsy Holden, a leading and well-respected citizen in Stony Point for decades would not let anything she owned become run down.

Then Annie thought of Grey Gables, how shabby the large old house had been when she first saw it after so many years away. Gram had grown old, and she eventually became unable to keep up with the house's needs. Annie had made progress on Grey Gables, but there was still so much to do. And now it seemed there was another property, one that was even worse? Oh, surely not.

"You know where this Fairview place is?" she asked Alice.

"Annie, of course I do! I've lived in Stony Point, forever, remember?"

She scrambled to her feet. "Then take me there."

Alice, still on the floor, gaped up at her. "Are you kidding? You mean right now?"

"Right now."

"But it's raining cats and dogs!"

"Then you may borrow my extra umbrella."

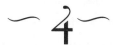

Rain pounded Alice's red Mustang like a thousand angry fists as the women drove out of town. The windshield wipers slashed with such a violent rhythm, Annie could hardly see the road in front of them.

"Why, oh, why did I let you talk me into this?" Alice said, squinting as she guided the car through the torrent. "I'm driving like an old lady, you know. A myopic, hands-frozen-to-the-steering-wheel, terrified old lady."

Annie felt a pang of guilt for giving in to the urge to look at Fairview immediately, and for coercing her best friend into driving her there in such dangerous weather conditions. The weatherman forecasted a clearing period in the next couple of days. She could have waited. But she didn't want to. Something compelled her to see the property Gram owned. Secretly owned, as it turned out.

She gazed out the passenger window to glimpse the drowned landscape. Water sprayed upward from the Mustang's tires in frantic waves as the car hissed along the pavement. Puddles had become miniature ponds, and bare brown tree branches wept from the relentless downpour.

"I just don't understand ... ." she murmured, and let her voice trail.

"You don't understand what? How it can rain this hard for so long, and we still haven't spotted Noah and his ark?

Or how I can be such a great big gullible sap for agreeing to go on this little excursion?"

Annie glanced at her friend.

"I don't understand how Gram could have owned another house but never mentioned it to me. We were so close at one time. We talked about everything. But she never so much as hinted at a second property in Maine. Did you see the date on that deed, Alice? That place has been hers for more than a quarter of a century, and never said a word about it."

Alice turned off the highway and followed a muddy narrow lane. She stopped the car when they reached a fallen limb imposing a barrier across the driveway.

"Well," she said grimly, "there it is for your viewing pleasure! Fairview."

Between each brief strike of the wiper blades, Annie caught glimpses of brown and gray, of something broken and sad. Of something that needed a loving touch.

Another old house to fix up, Annie thought.

Grey Gables had needed a loving touch, too; but that old house had been Gram's beloved home, full of familiar furniture, its nooks and crannies filled with bit and pieces of Gram's life.

Annie sighed. Instinct told her Fairview was in worse shape than Grey Gables ever had been.

"Well, let's see it." She grabbed the door handle.

"*What*? You're kidding, right? Do you realize this is mud season?"

"Not kidding. I know what season it is, but I want to see what the house is like."

"You mean up close and personal?" Alice gawked at her like Annie had just turned green and purple.

"Exactly. Here's your umbrella. You coming with me?"

"I am not getting out in this deluge to look at that old wreck. We'll come back another day."

"Suit yourself." Annie flung open the door. The rain greeted her with enthusiasm, and she was soaked before she had time to pop open her umbrella. She stepped into mud up to her ankles, grimaced at the cold squish, but pushed forward with resolve.

If I had any sense I'd come back later, she thought. *Guess I don't have any sense.*

By the time she had slogged through the gooey yard with its overgrown shrubbery and untended trees to the porch, Alice had caught up to her. The glower she fixed on Annie was anything but lovely.

"Did I know you could be this stubborn?" she yelled over the noise of rain pelting their umbrellas.

Annie smiled. "I just wanted to look around for a minute or two. You should have stayed in the car."

"Uh huh. Like I'm going to let you do this by yourself."

They gingerly mounted the two rotting wooden steps and picked their way across the sagging porch. Once beneath the porch roof, Annie lowered the umbrella and shook the rain off of it. Tracking the length of the house with her gaze, she followed the line of peeling paint on the windowsills and the cracked panes of glass they held. Mildew trailed along the walls as if it had a destination, adding another dimension to the weathered-gray siding. She turned and looked out at the dreary front yard, wondering what it might look like on a warm summer day if everything was trimmed and blooming with life.

But at the present moment it was, simply, Foulview. Yes. And it was so, so sad.

"Seen enough?" Alice asked hopefully.

Annie shook her head. "Not yet."

"You aren't going inside, are you?"

"Of course I am." She pulled out a tarnished set of keys from her pocket and dangled them like a bell between Alice and her. "If these unlock it."

Alice narrowed her eyes. "Those look oddly familiar … like a set of keys recently found in an old cedar chest from a certain person's attic."

"Yep. Sure 'nuff."

Alice chewed the inside of her lower lip, watching, and Annie could tell she was praying the door was locked so solid that no key would ever open it.

With cold, wet, clumsy fingers, Annie thrust one of the keys into the blackened brass knob and turned. There was a soft, gratifying snick. She twisted the knob then pushed the door.

Nothing. She pushed again. Once more the door did not yield. She frowned at the key and the knob.

That key had turned; she had heard the lock release its hold. She rattled the key, and then pushed again, harder, using all her weight.

"Lend me your shoulder, would you?" Annie asked, grunting as she shoved.

Alice sighed, but she gave in, pushing hard.

The door finally gave way with an awful screech of

protesting old hinges as it flung inward to bash itself against the wall. It came back toward them, but Annie caught it with the flat of her hand and pushed it fully open to reveal a dark interior. The odor of damp, mildew and mice greeted the women. Something sour hung in the air, as well. Sour and dirty.

"*Ewww!*" Alice said, waving her hand in front of her face. She took a step backward.

"Yes. Ewww." Annie took a step forward and crossed the threshold into the shadowy room.

"Turn on the lights." Annie suggested, lingering on the porch side of the open door.

"Right. *You* turn on the lights." She looked at her friend over her shoulder. "Do you honestly think there would be electricity hooked up after all these years?"

Alice pulled a face. "Light a candle?" she asked hopefully.

Annie squinted into the dimness, and made out the shapes of the windows. She walked to the nearest one.

"This place is worse than the attic at Grey Gables," Alice said, coming inside and shutting the door.

"You think?"

"Yes! *Way, way* worse."

Annie pulled back a curtain. The rotted fabric came apart in her hands. She went from window to window in the front room. The other old curtains fell to her touch and lay in dingy heaps on the floor. Gray daylight leaked in, as if it had to be coaxed through the filthy windows.

She and Alice silently surveyed the room. As dirty and filmy and covered with cobwebs as they were, the windows were lovely and large. Two of them were cracked but none broken out completely. Lumps of furniture huddled beneath protective sheets. Dusty pictures hung on the walls and numerous scars marked the old hardwood floors. Dead bugs and rodent droppings seemed to be everywhere they looked. A dried snakeskin near the fireplace made Annie shudder.

"Oh dear," she said, swallowing hard. "I surely hope we don't run into that skin's living owner."

"Ugh." Alice agreed. "Let's go home." She walked back to the front door, but Annie gathered her grit and forged ahead.

She opened a door just off the living room, revealing a bedroom with the bed made up as though expecting the owner to return for a nap. A dusty, quilted coverlet was spread over the top. Dustsheets were draped over the furniture in that room too. But that quilt caught her attention, and Annie wanted to examine it.

She crossed to the window on the other side of the room, and opened the tattered curtains. She turned to take a closer look at the quilt. Mice had used parts of it freely for nesting material, but the beauty of design remained. Each block was intricately cross-stitched with a flower of a different type and color. She touched one block with the tip of one finger and felt the coolness of the fabric and the roughness of the threaded pattern.

"Annie!" She jumped and looked over her shoulder. Alice stood in the doorway, arms folded. "Do you plan to look in every room of this old wreck?"

"I do."

A silence.

"Well, okay then," Alice said. Sighing and defeated, she approached. "Oh! Look at that!" She bent closer, and like

Annie, ran her fingertips across the quilt top. "Lovely work, by a real craftsman … or rather, craftswoman. But not Betsy, I'm sure."

"No. This is not Gram's style at all. I wonder if there's more." Annie glanced around.

Something rustled nearby, and she thought she saw movement.

"What was that?" Alice said, eyes wide, an edge in her voice.

Annie and Alice stood perfectly still, staring at the corner where the noise had come from.

"Annie," Alice whispered, "I truly hate mice. Big time!"

"Why, Alice!" Annie whispered back. "When I had mice in my attic, you didnt turn into a quivering mass of jelly."

Alice shrugged. "I know! Weird, huh? I admired myself for covering it up so well."

"Well, I'm sure that was not a mouse," Annie murmured back. "It was too loud, and too big."

"Too *big*? You mean you saw something?"

"Didn't you?"

"No!" Alice whisper-shrieked. "What did you see?"

"I don't know. Probably nothing. Probably my imagination." Though she had seen a flash of movement, and it had been much larger than a little mouse. She peered into the corner a moment longer, but saw nothing more and finally turned away. "Come on. I want to see the rest of the house." She walked to the doorway, but her friend seemed frozen in place. "Alice, it's not like you to be this timid."

Alice uttered a funny, shaky little laugh.

"Annie, I *hate* mice," she whispered. "I do not want to

see a mouse."

"I never knew you were such a big chicken."

Alice pulled up her backbone. "I'm not chicken!" she said stoutly. "I just … I just don't like mice, that's all."

"You want to wait on the front porch?"

Alice stared at her. She lifted her chin.

"What do you take me for? I'm in with you, girlfriend. Lead on." She gave Annie a weak smile. "Just do me a little favor, huh? Scare away the mice as you go."

Annie laughed and gave her friend a quick hug. "Thanks for making me laugh. I need it. Come on. I want to see the rest of my new house. You still with me?"

Alice shot a look around the room and then went to the door.

"Yep. No matter what else is in here."

They entered the short, broad hallway. Something cold shot across Annie with the unexpectedness of a lightning strike.

"Oh!" she gasped before she could stop herself.

"What?" Alice grabbed Annie's upper arm and dug her fingers into the muscle. "Did you see a mouse?"

"No." Annie's voice trailed as she looked at the front door. It was firmly closed, and so were all doors leading off the room and hallway. The windows were shut also. "I thought—"

She caught sight of her friend's face. Alice, always so full of fun and bravado, looked pale and nervous.

"Nothing. I just thought of something I have to do when I get home, that's all."

Alice thinned her lips. "Well, for goodness sake! Don't holler like that unless you mean it. You scared me."

"Maybe we should just go on home," Annie said. "I'll fix us some tea—"

"Nothing doing. You dragged me out here to this old ruin, and we're not leaving until we've seen it."

Now that was more like the Alice MacFarlane Annie knew!

Annie opened the next door off the hallway, revealing a small bathroom, with necessary but unremarkable white facilities; it had standard white tiles and no covering over the small window. Next was a bedroom. She went straight to the window and opened the curtains.

Alice said, "I'll open the rest of them in the other rooms. More light in this place can't hurt."

Moments later, Annie heard the sound of old fabric ripping as Alice made the rounds. With the windows exposed, the inside of the cottage lightened up, even though the dreary afternoon sky outside provided only weak light.

The second and third bedrooms were similar to the first, a bit smaller, with furniture under dustcovers and a Jack-and-Jill half-bath between the two. The women found a dining room at the back of the house, complete with table and chairs, uncovered, dust-laden, and mismatched.

"This kitchen has seen better days," Annie said as they crossed from the dining room into the kitchen.

"Yeah. Like back in 1941. Look at this old black and white tile. It's cool, in a way, and so are those ancient appliances, but—"

She broke off as they heard an odd sound, almost a moan.

"What was *that*?" Annie said, her eyes as big as Alice's

this time.

"I don't know, but it sounded awful, like someone is sick."

"Or injured." Annie added as she stepped into the hallway. "Hello? Is someone here?"

The women stood immobile, ears straining. They heard nothing but rain pounding the roof.

"An owl, maybe," Alice offered.

"In the daytime?"

"Yeah, well, I'd rather think it's an owl than—" Alice stopped speaking, shivered a little and said, "Have you seen enough of Foulview yet?"

"Than what? Alice, what were going to say? You'd rather think it's an owl than what? Hey, come back here!" Annie trotted after her friend who had reached the front door by that time. "You'd rather think it's an owl than what?"

"Than nothing." Umbrella unfurled and held aloft, Alice was already striding to the Mustang. She hollered over her shoulder, "I'm leaving. You coming with?" She glanced over the car roof at Annie, and then she opened the driver's door and got inside.

Annie blew out a big breath.

"Well, I guess I am 'coming with' if I don't want to swim home," she muttered peevishly to herself. She closed the front door, tugging it hard to snug it into the swollen frame, and then locked it. Popping open the other umbrella, she grimaced and stepped out into the rain and the mud.

She could not shake the feeling that someone, or something, watched her leave.

— 5 —

Along with its old architecture, good restaurants, and rugged, rocky Atlantic shoreline, Stony Point also could very well be listed in an encyclopedia somewhere as a hotbed of gossip. Many little things reminded Annie of this detail several times the next day.

When she woke up that morning, she opened her eyes to welcome sunshine for the first time in more than a week. The golden light poured into her bedroom windows and she got up with new-found energy and fresh purpose. That day, she wanted to put away all that yarn still piled up in the living room. But first she had a few errands to run, so while she was in town, she would try to find out something about Fairview. Surely someone knew something about the place. Maybe she would even make another trip out there.

She fixed herself a quick bowl of cold cereal, fed Boots her favorite kibble and then went upstairs to shower. The bright sunlight outside did not fool Annie into believing the day was as warm as a spring morning in Texas. She dressed in dark green slacks, and a green and white-striped oxford shirt. A camel brown jacket and brown loafers completed her outfit.

As Annie put the finishing touches on her makeup, she looked hard into the mirror at the face that stared back.

"You have moped enough for the entire year," she said

to the woman in the mirror. "I want you to be productive today! First, take the Malibu to get the oil changed, and don't forget to talk to the mechanic about why it's been running rough lately. Then go to the post office. Do *not* forget to stop at the hardware store for some penetrating oil for those old hinges on the cedar chest, and last but not least, pop in at A Stitch in Time." She paused, gave her reflection a baleful look and added, "And for goodness sake, Annie Dawson, stop talking to yourself!"

She heard a sound from outside, a muffled noise like the slamming of a car door. She crossed to the window and looked out. Sure enough, she had an unexpected guest. Emma Watson was trotting up the front walk, her Avon sample bag in hand.

Although Annie had not expected Emma that day, she was out of a few products and had been meaning to call the woman. She hurried downstairs and reached the front door just as Emma did.

"Good morning!" said the heavyset, gray-haired sales rep. "Lovely day, isn't it? After all that rain?"

"Oh, yes, absolutely lovely." Annie held open the door to admit the woman. "I'm so happy to see some sun. Please come in, Emma. May I get you some coffee?"

Emma entered the house in a fragrant cloud and gave Annie a big smile. Annie noted how the woman's makeup always looked flawless and newly applied. She supposed if one was a representative for a cosmetics company, one did a better job of selling if the products were displayed on a living palette.

"No, thanks. I think I've had my limit of coffee already

this morning. I just thought I'd check and see if you need anything." She glanced around the usually tidy living room. Behind the lens of her large glasses, her eyes widened at the array of yarn Annie had yet to put away. "My goodness, Annie! What did you do? Hold up A Stitch in Time?"

Annie laughed and cleared a pile of skeins from their place on the sofa so she and Emma could sit down. She indicated all the yarn and thread with a sweep of her hand.

"All of this is a gift from my daughter."

Emma looked at it all again, and then said, "Well, it's easy to see you're going to be busy." She settled onto the sofa and put her bag on the floor. "What are you working on now?"

Annie fetched the runner from her tote and smoothed it out for Emma to examine.

"Such intricate stitches and tiny thread! Oh, I do envy your patience and your talent!"

"I'd be happy to teach you some time, if you ever want to learn."

Emma chuckled and shook her head.

"I would love that, Annie, but I am all thumbs, I'm afraid. Besides, selling Avon and taking care of my husband and grandson keeps me plenty busy."

"Do you sell Avon all over Stony Point?"

"My dear," she said with a smile, "there is something you should know about me: I sell to anyone who wants to buy—here, there, or anywhere!"

She started to reach into her bag, but Annie stopped her.

"Emma, how long have you lived here?"

"In Stony Point? Most of my adult life."

"Did you ever meet anyone named Joseph and Alta Harper?"

"Joseph and Alta Harper, you said?" Emma frowned as she thought about it. "No. Those names don't ring a bell. Why?"

Annie knew from her past experience with Emma that the woman frequently passed along news and gossip. While Annie wanted to know more about Fairview and its previous owners, the fact that her grandmother had the deed to the place seemed peculiar, especially given the degree to which Fairview had deteriorated. She preferred to let no one else know about the deed. At least, not until she had more information.

Annie waved her hand airily. "I overheard someone mention them and wondered who they were," she said vaguely.

She watched as curiosity began to brew in Emma's sharp eyes. Before the woman could pry, Annie looked down with eagerness at the product bag on the floor by Emma's feet.

"So, what good buys do you have for this campaign? I'm glad you stopped by, because I'm out of nearly everything!"

The tactic worked. Emma launched into an enthusiastic sales pitch, and Annie cheerfully ordered more products than she could use in the foreseeable future.

After Emma left, Annie grabbed her purse and car keys, and headed into town.

Sticking with her itinerary, she dropped the car off at Powell's Auto Service for the oil change.

"Would you look it over, please?" she said as she handed the keys over to a man who wore a shirt with the name "Mac" stitched above the pocket. "It seems to be 'jerky' lately."

"'Jerky'?" Mac asked, frowning slightly.

"Yes. Not running as smoothly as it usually does."

"Well, lady, that ain't hardly a new car you got there." He dipped his head toward the Malibu.

She bristled at the blunt comment. The car had been a Christmas gift from Wayne; she had cherished and cared for it carefully. The way this man talked, one would think it was nothing more than a rust-bucket held together with tape and chewing gum.

Now, Annie, she thought, *he never said any such thing.*

It was almost as if Wayne's voice spoke out loud, and a shiver danced over her skin. He had always been so reasonable, so quietly logical. And that imaginary voice was right. For that matter, so was the mechanic. The Malibu was not new. In fact, it had lost its newness long ago.

She smiled at Mac in his grease-stained blue uniform. "If you will just look at it, please."

"Be glad to," he said. "But I got a couple of others ahead of yours. Gonna be a while."

"Oh? How long?"

He shrugged. "Not sure. A while."

She had not expected to be in a waiting queue. Well, no help for it now. She would just have to take her time with the errands.

"Here." She scribbled her phone number on a scrap of paper from her purse. "That's my cell phone. Will you call me?"

He nodded, absently stuffed the paper in his shirt pocket and walked back to the garage. Annie sighed, and then went outside.

Well, she thought, *if I have to be without wheels, this is a good day for it.*

She stood for a moment, taking in a deep, fresh breath. The sea air was chilly, but the sun was warm against her face. She smiled and set off.

Her next stop was the post office to pick up a book of stamps. The woman behind the counter looked over her half-glasses when Annie entered. Her gray hair was shorter than usual and tightly curled.

"Good morning, Norma. You doing okay today?"

"Yup."

"Looks like you got a new perm."

"Get one every four months. Never have liked fussin' with my hair."

She eyed Annie's gray-blond hair critically, but said nothing.

Annie patted her chin length pageboy and murmured, "I probably need a trim myself."

Norma merely blinked.

Annie added, "I'm out of stamps."

The woman waited silently.

"I'd like to buy a book of them, please."

Norma took the stamps from a drawer beneath the counter. She passed them halfway across the counter, and then stopped, fingertips protecting the booklet. The expression in her eyes was more than a little flinty.

"This post office takes care of our own. Your mail carrier would have taken that box right into the house for you."

"I beg your pardon?"

"I said your mail carrier would have taken that box right into the house for you."

Annie took a step back and stared at the woman. Stony

Point had its own way of passing news, and Annie had witnessed it firsthand many times, but this was a little weird. How did Norma know about the big box and the reluctant deliveryman? Annie narrowed her eyes.

"Have you been talking to Alice MacFarlane?" she asked.

"Not lately."

Norma shoved the stamps the rest of the way across the counter. Annie picked them up and slipped them into her purse.

"Then how did you know … ?"

Norma rubbed her nose with the back of her hand, probed her inner jaw with her tongue and squinted a little over the top of her glasses.

"Because Peggy Carson told me about the gift from your daughter. It stands to reason with all that yarn, the box it came in was too big to go through your door."

"But how did you—"

"You've not paid me for those stamps yet."

Without taking her eyes off the woman across the counter, Annie fished her wallet from her purse. She pulled out a ten dollar bill and silently handed it over.

"That other delivery service in town never takes anythin' inside for anyone," Norma said sourly. "Never. It's always best to trust the people you know."

"Why, Norma, I did not—"

"The post office has been in business since Benjamin Franklin, but do folks use us nowadays?" Norma raised her voice. "No! They use e-mail and Facebook and Twitter. They mail packages through all sorts of Johnnycome-lately delivery services and just forget all about the post office! Here's your change."

Annie backed away from the counter and nearly collided with a harried young mother with two blonde-haired toddlers in tow.

Sometimes, Norma could be downright peculiar, but today, with that strange look in her eyes, the woman could also be a little frightening.

Don't be silly, Annie told herself. *This is Norma. Good, hard-working, no-nonsense Norma. A Stony Point institution.*

"See you later," she blurted, and then dashed out the door, away from that inscrutable, unnerving gaze.

Once she was outside again, Annie stood a moment. She gathered her thoughts and brushed away the incident. She had too many things to do that day to let Norma's odd behavior bother her.

She glanced at her watch, knowing the car wouldn't be ready for a while yet, and although the hour was a little early for lunch, that was all right with her. At least the diner would not be too crowded, and the walk there would be pleasant.

These days, inside The Cup & Saucer, the customers no longer gave Annie long perusals full of curiosity and speculation the way they did when she first moved to Stony Point. She had lived in small-town Maine long enough by now that her face, if not her name, was becoming familiar.

Along the far end of the diner's dining room, three tables had been pushed together, and it appeared as though a city government delegation was having a luncheon meeting. At the head of the table, Mayor Ian Butler glanced up. He caught Annie's eye, smiled a silent greeting, held her gaze a moment, and then became all business again as he turned back to the well-dressed men and women around the tables. An alderman and the city clerk looked at Annie, then at each other and shared what seemed to Annie to be a knowing smile.

Annie felt her face grow hot. It was no secret in Stony Point that Ian liked her more than a little. If the truth be known, she liked him too. A lot. But that's where it stopped. Wayne's absence had left a giant hole in her heart that still ached on a daily basis. At this point in her life, Annie was in no way ready to fill that void. Being a widower himself, Ian probably was not any more ready for a serious relationship than Annie was. He had been devoted to his late wife, and her death from a brain aneurism had devastated him as hard as Wayne's heart attack had hit Annie. For now, at least in Annie's estimation, it was best for the two of them just to be friends.

She dragged her gaze from the table of city officials and their knowing smiles. Her eyes fell on Max and Mabel Cline, an elderly couple she had met at Stony Point Community Church. Weathered by age, the pair was gray-haired and stooped, but bright eyed, sharp witted, and friendly. She paused by their table long enough to say hello and inquire about their health.

As she seated herself near the window to enjoy her solitary lunch, Annie reminded herself that since Max and Mabel were some of Stony Point's oldest citizens and lifelong residents, they might know something of interest about Fairview. But right then, she remained steadfast in commitment to keep the deed a secret. If the elderly couple did not leave The Cup & Saucer before she did, Annie would talk to them.

Right then she looked up to greet Peggy, who arrived at the table with a glass of ice water and a menu.

"Hey, Annie," she said. "You by yourself today?"

Annie nodded.

"I'm getting the oil changed on the Malibu. The fellow had a couple of other customers ahead of me, so it will be a little while.

"And you thought you'd drop in for lunch. Good idea."

"Right. So how is the egg salad today?"

"It's delicious, of course." Peggy grinned. "Do we serve anything that isn't?"

"Nothing I have had so far. I love the food here. Can you bring me some sweet gherkins with that sandwich?"

"Yup. And coffee?"

"And coffee."

Peggy started to move away, but Annie stopped her.

"Uh, Peggy, may I ask you something?"

"Sure. What do you want to know?

"By any chance did you happen to say anything to Norma at the post office about the gift LeeAnn sent to me?"

"Sure did! Wow, Annie! You must be so excited. I'd love to see what she sent to you."

"You are more than welcome to drop by and look at it. But, tell me, what did you say to Norma?"

Perhaps the question came out more brusquely than Annie intended. A flash of confusion shot across Peggy's round, sweet face.

"Just that you said you got a huge shipment of yarn from LeeAnn. Why?"

At that moment, Annie realized that her friend had not

been gossiping, but merely passing along good news. She silently scolded herself for being so touchy. After all, good news ought to be shared.

"No reason." She smiled broadly, apologetically. "Listen, would you bring me some apple pie with that sandwich, too, please?"

"Shall do—a la mode?"

Annie pondered for just a moment. "Sure! Why not?"

She watched Peggy sashay cheerfully toward the kitchen. She was glad she had given Peggy's husband, Wally, the job of renovating Grey Gables. He had worked hard, been dependable, and his price was fair. There had been so much to do on that old house Annie never would have been able to tackle it all on her own. Unfortunately, as much as she didn't like the notion, Annie might have to do the same thing to Fairview. If so, hiring Wally would be a high priority. Plus, she liked knowing she was helping the Carson family.

When Peggy brought her sandwich and coffee, Annie asked her in an undertone, "Did Norma seem … odd to you when you saw her?"

"Odd?"

"Yes. Snappish, touchy."

"Oh, that. Yes. She's a little upset, and I can understand why. Some tourist told her a day or two ago that with all the new technology and services available, the post office is becoming obsolete and ought to be shut down completely in the next few years. Especially a post office as small as ours."

"Oh, no! Poor Norma. No wonder she was so out of sorts. She loves that job."

"And really, she has nothing to worry about. Just be extra

nice when you see her, would you, Annie? She needs our friendship and support."

Annie smiled. "I'll do that."

She had planned to send some of that big Avon order she had made earlier in a gift to LeeAnn, so she would use the post office when the time came. And she would buy some extra stamps at the same time.

This was just one more reason she loved Stony Point. Everyone seemed to care about one another—it was like Brookfield in that way.

Dressed in similar dark blue fleece tracksuits, the elderly Clines were finishing their pie by the time Annie had finished hers. She stopped by their table on the way to the cash register and received a warm greeting.

"You look prettier every time I see you, young lady," Max told her, shaking her hand with a grip that belied his age.

"Why, Max!" she laughed. "Thank you."

"He's over eighty, and my husband still likes to flirt," Mabel said, chuckling. She squeezed Annie's fingers lightly with her own cool, frail-looking ones. "But he's right, Annie. You do add a bright spot to Stony Point. Would you like to sit?"

"Can we buy you a piece of pie or some coffee?" Max offered.

"Oh, thank you, no. I just finished some a moment ago. They make good pie here, though, don't they?"

"Almost as good as Mabel's," Max said. "Almost. Have a seat, anyway."

Annie took an empty seat at their table, feeling cozy beneath their friendly regard.

"Thank you. And I won't stay long, but I was hoping you could answer something for me."

"What's that?" Max said. He picked up his cup, took a drink and met her eyes over the rim.

"What do you know about an old place outside of town called Fairview?"

Mabel looked thoughtful and stared off at nothing. Max screwed up his face and scratched his chin.

"Well, I don't know much," Mabel said after a bit. "I know it was once a lovely place, but no one has ever lived in it for long."

"I seem to remember someone living there for a short time, oh, about ten, twenty, maybe thirty years ago. Don't think anyone lives there now, though." Max looked at her. "Why do you ask?"

In light of their open regard and harmless interest, Annie had to remind herself not to spill more information than she should by getting caught up in her own need for information.

"Right now, I'm just curious more than anything else. Do you know anything about the owners?"

Max playfully wagged a finger at her. "I hear tell you like to solve curiosities and mysteries. That old place is sure ripe for that."

"Yes, it is. But, about the owners … ?"

"My dear," said Mabel, "I can't tell you for sure, but I think the owner of Fairview lives somewhere else. In fact, I don't think he ever did live here, did he, Max?"

The old man shook his head. "I really don't know. Tell you the truth, I just never gave that place much thought or interest one way or the other."

"Was the owner's name Harper?"

"If I ever knew the name, I don't know it now." Mabel looked at her husband. "How about you, dear? You've always had a better memory than me."

But Max shook his head. "No, don't know what the name was."

Annie listened to the exchange with dismay, realizing this was simply one more dead end in her quest. If anyone in Stony Point would have had firsthand knowledge of Fairview and its owner or owners, she thought this aged couple would be the ones. She hid her disappointment behind a bright smile.

"Well, as I said, I was just curious," she said. "If you think of anything, please call me, will you?"

To wipe away the Clines's curiosity, Annie changed the subject, and they chatted a few more minutes about weather and hopes for a lovely garden when the weather cooperated. After leaving The Cup & Saucer, she strolled to Malone's Hardware where she searched the shelves for penetrating oil.

"Hello there, Annie," Mike Malone said, striding up to her. She could never look at Mike with his lithe, wiry build without thinking of an energetic athlete, a runner perhaps. "May I help you find something?"

"Hi, Mike. Yes, I think you can. I have an old cedar chest that is just lovely—one of Gram's old treasures, of course—but the hinges are rusted and stiff. I don't want to damage that beautiful wood, so what's the best oil to use on those hinges?"

"Well, now." He surveyed the selection, squinting a

little, and then pulled out a pair of readers from his shirt pocket and settled them on his nose. "Gettin' old, Annie. Can't see a thing up close anymore."

She laughed. "I'm sure I'll be at that point soon enough. It seems I have more gray hair every day."

He grinned, running the flat of his hand over his head. "Well, mine is still as brown as it ever was, but I'm *losing* more of it every day, seems like." He picked up a small can with a thin, pointed applicator from the shelf. "Right here. This is what you need. Won't hurt the wood, and it'll work good on all hinges—doors, cabinets, what have you."

"Will work on old locks too?" she asked, thinking of the creaky old lock on Fairview's front door.

"Yup. Locks too."

"Thanks. And it's small enough that it won't take up a lot of space."

"As if you have to worry about space at Grey Gables."

Mike was known to be a fount of local history, so as she walked to the cash register with him, Annie said, in what she hoped was on offhand manner, "Say, Mike, did you ever meet anyone named Joseph and Alta Harper?"

He went around to the other side of the counter.

"No," he said, slowly furrowing his brow as he thought about it. "Can't say that I ever did. They aren't from around here, are they?"

She shook her head. "I don't think so, but I'm not sure. I was hoping you could tell me."

He narrowed his eyes in thought, tugged on his left ear for a moment, and finally shook his head. "Nope. Sorry. Those names just do not ring a bell."

He punched in the price of the oil on the cash register. "Anything else for you today, Annie?"

"Just the oil. What about Fairview?" she asked.

The cash register calculated what she owed.

"That'll be five dollars, even. What do you mean, 'what about Fairview?'"

She gave him the five dollars, and said, "I mean, what do you know about it?"

"Well, I know it was built in the twenties as a vacation home for some fellow ... I've forgotten his name or the details, but I tell you what. I have that information somewhere. I'll dig it up, and give you a call when I find it."

"That'd be great, Mike. Thank you!"

He put the oil in a small brown sack and handed it to her.

"Why the interest in that old place?" he asked.

"Oh, just curious."

"Well, don't let your curiosity lead you into mischief or anything dangerous, Annie. That old place has been deserted for a long time. It's really run down and best left alone."

She started to ask for clarification but a harried-looking, red-faced man rushed up to the counter, interrupting their conversation by saying, "Mike, I got a big leak in the kitchen, and I need some pipe—ASAP!"

"I'll be right with you, Howard. You already shut the water off, right? Annie, I'll give you a call." He came around the counter and walked with Howard back toward plumbing supplies.

She wondered what Mike had meant, though, when he had said, with a sense of foreboding, "That place is best left alone."

~6~

"Annie Dawson! What are you doing here?" Mary Beth called from the back of the store as Annie walked into A Stitch in Time. "Don't tell me you've used up all that yarn already?"

Annie laughed as Mary Beth approached. "Hardly. I've not even put it all away yet."

"Hi, Annie," Kate said from behind the counter as she hung up the phone. "Isn't it a lovely day?"

"Oh my, yes! Especially after all the rain."

Mary Beth said, "You look a little … um … troubled. What's wrong?"

Annie waved one hand dismissively.

"Not troubled, exactly. But I just got a phone call a minute ago from the mechanic over at Powell's Auto Service. He said the Malibu's timing belt has slipped a tooth and he doesn't have one in stock. Plus, he thinks the fuel injectors are clogged and need to be flushed."

Mary Beth made a face. "Tough break. I hate car trouble just about more than anything I can think of."

"Who doesn't!" Kate said, nodding.

"Well, it is no fun, that's for sure," Annie said.

"I truly wish I knew more about auto mechanics than I do," Kate said, "but I hardly know anything. They could tell me my car's bilge pipe needed new socks, and I would probably believe them."

Annie laughed at that. "Well, if it's any comfort, Kate, I know for a certainty that cars do not have bilge pipes or socks. Thank goodness my years at the dealership taught me a little something. But the sad part is, I have to leave the car at the garage until it's fixed."

Mary Beth gave Annie a sympathetic look.

"So you're stranded," she said.

"Oh, not really," Annie replied. "Not unless I want to be stuck, anyway. It will take a few days for the part to come in, then another day or so for the work to be done. But the thing is, Stony Point is so small that nothing is really very far from anything else. I can always walk to where I want to go."

"Don't you just love it?" Mary Beth grinned. "Isn't this just the best little town ever?"

"It's great here. I like it better all the time."

"And people here like you, Annie," Mary Beth said warmly. You're an asset to this community. Betsy would be so proud of you."

"Now, Annie, don't get all embarrassed," Kate said, laughing a little. "Mary Beth, you made her blush!"

"Oh, I'm just being silly," Annie said, shaking her head. She had been so gloomy and lonely for the last few days that their friendly words touched that spot in her that was still tender. "It's good to know that Stony Pointers like me."

"Stony Pointers?" Mary Beth and Kate echoed at the same time; then they laughed.

"That's a good one, Annie," Kate said.

"Y'all are just too sweet," she told them. Then, before she could get weepy and foolish, she said, "Would you believe that in all my patterns, including the new ones from LeeAnn, I do not have a single slipper pattern?"

"Well, we can help you." Kate said. "I have that pattern I mentioned at the meeting the other day. And I've already started a design of my own. Plus, Annie, I found the cutest patterns in this book."

She picked up a crochet pattern book, opened the page and put her finger on the photograph of some comfy-looking brown slippers with high cuffs.

"Look! Aren't these darling? They sorta look like boots, don't they? And those buttons on the side add a little something."

"I love those slippers! They look so snug and warm. Men or women either one could wear them."

"There is this pattern also." Kate turned the page, and showed a pair of striped slippers in white and two shades of pink.

"Aren't they the sweetest things you've ever seen?" Annie exclaimed. "Oh, I want to make both patterns. What fun! I can't wait to get started."

The three women looked through the rest of the book together, exclaiming over the variety of slipper patterns.

"Well," Annie said, when they closed the book, "since I'm walking, I better get going. I want to buy this book. And I'm going to sit down tonight and start a pair of these slippers."

"What about the table runner?"

"What about it? I'll work on it too. Never let it be said that Annie Dawson let grass grow under her crochet hook!"

~ 7 ~

Despite her assurances to Kate and Mary Beth, without access to her car Annie nursed a niggling bit of unease that she might feel trapped and lonely at Grey Gables. But, once she was home, she dismissed the foolish notion and dove headlong into the final organization of her new yarns and threads. In the attic, she located three large, stackable wicker baskets. Of course, more of Gram's keepsakes filled those spaces.

By the time Annie had sorted, laundered and given away the clothes and memorabilia that Gram had stored in the baskets, baked three pies for the church pie supper, called LeeAnn twice and crocheted both pairs of slippers, the week had slipped past.

When she was able to retrieve the Malibu, it ran good as new, and she sent up a little prayer of thanks for her good fortune as she drove to the post office on Tuesday morning in another chilly gray drizzle. She wanted to talk with Norma before going to the Hook and Needle Club meeting.

She had arisen earlier than usual that morning and made her special recipe of chocolate-chip cookies. She was feeling a touch queasy from eating so much of the raw cookie dough, and then indulging in several cookies fresh from the oven. The ones that remained were still warm inside the eight-by-eight-inch plastic container she carried into the post office.

A line consisting of three men, two women and a teen-aged girl were queued at the counter. Norma stood on the other side, passively and efficiently weighing packages, selling postage, filling out paperwork, adding an extra stamp to an envelope. She hardly spoke, only to answer questions, and she never smiled. The line moved, and when it was Annie's turn, three more postal customers stood behind her, waiting to be helped.

"Good morning, Norma," Annie said warmly as she stepped up to the counter.

Norma inclined her head once. Annie put the plastic container on the countertop. The fragrance of chocolate wafted up, escaping from the tight lid.

"You are really busy today," she said to Norma. "Is it usually this busy in here?"

Norma briefly glanced behind Annie. The post office door opened and another person joined the queue.

"Usually," Norma replied, cutting her gaze away from the newcomer and back to Annie. "How can I help you today?"

"It's not what you can do for me today," Annie told her, "but it's what I want to do for you."

Norma's expression turned more suspicious than curious. "How's that?" she said.

"Well, I just want to let you know I appreciate all the time and hard work you have devoted to the post office all these years." Norma's expression did not change, so Annie continued. "In fact, I think everyone appreciates you."

"I do!" said the man behind Annie. "Where else could I buy stamps in Stony Point?"

Norma blinked at him.

"Yes," Annie said, smiling at the man. "Yes, we need the post office, and we need Norma. Right?" She glanced at the others in the line.

"Yes!"

"Right!"

She turned back to Norma. "Please don't listen to the foolish comments by tourists who don't know you or Stony Point, or how much Stony Pointers need this post office. We may use e-mail and Facebook and Twitter, and all the rest of it, but we'll always need the post office. And if anyone ever tries to take it away from us, we'll protest. Loud and long." She looked at the others. "Right?"

They all looked a little confused but backed her up with enthusiastic support.

"See?"

"Well, now," Norma said, gawking at everyone. "Well, now."

Annie laughed softly. "You don't need to say a word, Norma. But just don't worry about anything."

Norma let out a deep breath. "Why, Annie. Thank you for saying so. I guess you heard what that man said."

"Yes. But you just ignore it. And here." She pushed the container of cookies across the counter. "These are for you, just to say thanks for being so trustworthy." She glanced at her watch. "Goodness. I'm going to be late. See you later, Norma. Bye-bye."

"Goodbye," Norma said, still looking as if she had been poleaxed, but some life seemed to be returning to her eyes at last. "And thank you, Annie. This means a lot."

Annie gave her a smile and hurried outside. She truly

was going to be late. In fact, the meeting was probably getting under way right then.

That day was chilly and overcast, with the prediction of snow underscoring the weather forecast, and the store was bright and warm when Annie arrived. She sat in her usual seat.

"Sometimes," Kate said, thoughtfully after everyone seemed to be settled and began to pull projects from carrybags and totes, "I think I'd like to live somewhere in the South. You know, where the weather is warm most of the time, and where the winters are usually quite short."

"Maybe Annie will take you on a trip down to Texas some time," Stella said.

Kate smiled and said, "I was actually thinking of Florida." Everyone laughed, and she hurried to add, "Not that I wouldn't want to see Texas, of course. I mean, cowboys and horses and oil wells and all that, but Vanessa really would like to see Disney World."

"Honey," Annie said, slathering on her accent like butter on a hot biscuit, "if y'all want to go along with me to see cowboys and horses and oil wells and all that, you just come on ahead. We don't have Disney World, but we got Six Flags."

Kate grinned at her. "That would be uber-awesome."

"That would be what?" Mary Beth and Stella said in unison.

"Oh, that's something Vanessa uses a lot lately. It means super-duper."

"Now *that* I understand," Stella said, nodding. "In my day the word was 'swell'."

"And for us, it was 'groovy,'" Mary Beth said, and Gwen added. "Or 'cool.'"

"For us, it was 'rad' or 'radical,'" Kate said. "Or 'awesome.'"

"Yeah," Peggy said, "or 'gnarly.'"

"Heaven help us," Stella muttered, looking at Peggy as if she could hardly believe what she was hearing. "Where do you kids get these words? Whatever happened to words like 'nice' or 'lovely' or even 'terrific'?"

Alice said, "Well, Annie and I used to make up words. Remember, girlfriend? 'Sarcious' meant great and 'grimple' meant really bad."

"I had forgotten all about that!" Annie laughed. "Well, take a look, and see if you think these are sarcious, or if they're grimple."

From her tote, she lifted out the soft gray boot-style slippers and the delicate-looking striped ones with tiny rosettes on the toes that she had completed. The slippers made the circle with each woman examining the style and the stitches.

"These are wonderful, Annie!" Gwen said. "Sarcious!"

"Sarcious!" they all agreed, laughing.

"Well, I hate to admit it, but I've not even started on mine yet," Stella confessed after the group settled down again.

Mary Beth looked at the other women.

"Has anyone else made, or started, any slippers for the residents of Seaside Living other than Annie? And of course, Kate."

"I've got a good start on one," Gwen said. "Stella and I are getting together later this week to help each other."

"I've been looking on the Internet for a good pattern,"

Alice said. "You will be happy to know that I have narrowed it down to twelve."

"*Twelve?!*" two or three ladies echoed.

"We all know Alice," Peggy said. "If anyone can cross-stitch a dozen different pairs of slippers, it's Alice. She's got more energy than ten women half her age."

"Hey!" Alice said, a look of mock-annoyance on her face. "I'm not sure if that's a compliment or not."

Peggy laughed, and Alice shrugged, grinning.

"Oh, well," she said. "I'll take compliments when I can get them, even the backhanded ones."

After a bit of chuckling and twittering died down, Mary Beth said, "I take it then that we are all still on board with the slipper campaign?"

"Yes!"

"Absolutely."

"Why not?"

"You betcha."

Satisfied, Mary Beth sat down in the chair closest to the counter with the telephone and picked up part of a slipper she had been crocheting. Hers was a simple single crochet stitch pattern with dark red yarn, tightly worked and sturdy.

"So, Annie, what did you do with all your yarn and thread?" the store owner asked after a bit.

All the women looked at Annie, waiting for her reply, but their hands never stopped moving. Stella's and Gwen's knitting needles clicked, catching the glint of the store's lights. Peggy made careful, tiny stitches in the quilted top for one of a colorful pair of slippers. Alice's needle seemed to fly through the yellow gingham picture frame, eager to get it finished before her cousin's baby arrived. She had decided to make a series of three frames: an oval, an oblong, and a heart-shaped, and the project was almost finished.

"I found a lovely old cedar chest in the attic," Annie told the group.

Gwen stopped knitting to sigh and say wistfully, "Oh, I do so love cedar chests! I had one when I was girl … goodness, I wonder where it is now? I have not seen that lovely old chest in years."

"It's probably somewhere in Annie's attic," Alice said drily. There was the briefest of silences as this comment sunk in, and then the women broke into loud laughter.

"Good one, Alice!" Peggy said, clapping her hands.

"Betsy always was a pack rat," Gwen said. "If you gave her anything, no matter how small, years later she would dig it out of box or a drawer, if it was not already on display somewhere. I doubt that woman ever threw anything away."

Annie smiled, nodding.

"I think you're one hundred percent right, Gwen. I do believe I have found every Christmas and birthday card Hallmark ever made."

Again the women laughed.

"Everyone loved Betsy, and they loved to give her gifts," Alice said. "She was always so appreciative and gracious."

"That's true," Mary Beth murmured.

The group worked in companionable silence for a while before Kate, who usually stayed behind the counter during the meetings, carried her current project to the center of the group and held it up. It was a beautiful lacy dress of the palest lavender shade.

The women gasped in admiration, and Annie felt the tiniest twinge of envy. She loved her own style of crochet, but Kate possessed a rare gift: She was able to translate an image in her head to a material object for everyone to enjoy.

"I made this for Vanessa," Kate said softly. "I hope she likes it."

"How could she not?" Annie asked, leaning forward to examine the dress with her fingertips. The tiny scallops and shells, and the delicate picot stitches gave texture and grace to the entire garment. "Oh, Kate," she sighed. "I just love your work."

"Thank you, Annie," Kate said. "I consider that high praise. You do such lovely work yourself."

They put their heads together, each studying the other's work-in-progress.

Peggy cleared her throat loudly. "If you two are through founding Stony Point's first Mutual Admiration Society, I have a question." Peggy looked pointedly at Annie. "I think I speak for all of us when I ask, what intriguing thing did you find in that old cedar chest?"

"Yes, what?" Mary Beth and Gwen said in unison. Stella merely smiled and waited for the answer.

"Oh, just what you'd expect," she replied as she busied herself with her hook and yarn and refused to meet anyone's eyes. "Letters, cards, an old book or two. An old Bible with no inscription. There were some lovely silk scarves, though. Alice is going to use them for her Princessa parties."

In the chair next to Annie, Alice squirmed and gave her a meaningful glance, but Annie pretended not to see.

Instead she held up her piece, examined a few stitches

and asked, in what she hoped was an offhand way, "Please excuse me for changing the subject, but has anyone here ever heard of Joseph and Alta Harper?"

"Didn't he sell insurance door-to-door for a while?" Kate said.

"No," Mary Beth said, "that was John Hartley. Whatever happened to him, I wonder? I never did think he was much of a salesman. He sort of approached his potential customers with 'you wouldn't happen to need any insurance, would you?' Well, that attitude will not sell snowballs on a hot day."

"Who are these Harper people you're asking about?" Stella said, looking sharply at Annie.

"I was hoping someone could tell me."

"I've never heard of them," Gwen said.

"Ah *ha!*" Peggy said loudly, dropping her quilt piece into her lap to point at Annie. A gleam shone in her eyes. "You *did* find something in the attic, didn't you? Something that has to do with this Joseph and Alma Harper."

Annie crimped her mouth. She had hoped no one would notice her too clumsy segue from attic treasures to the identities of the Harpers.

"It's Alta, not Alma. And I just saw their names on something, that's all."

Peggy never took her eyes off Annie. Neither did Stella or Alice. Even Kate stared at her with open curiosity.

"Well you know, now that I think about it, I'm like you, Mary Beth. I wonder whatever did happen to John Hartley," Gwen said, her gaze focused on the project in her hands. She didn't see the others gawking at Annie. But her statement effectively, if temporarily, took the spotlight off of the younger woman.

From the look on Alice's face, though, Annie knew her good friend and neighbor would be unable to keep the Fairview deed a secret much longer. Annie sent her a pleading look, but Alice smiled blandly, as if she did not pick up on the clue.

For a while the women speculated about John Hartley, his whereabouts and his success, and any family he might have had, but Alice was a bulldog that morning, not easily distracted.

"Do you guys know anything about Fairview?" she asked, nonchalantly running floss through the yellow fabric of her frame-cover.

"That old place?" Kate said. "As Vanessa would say, *ewww!*"

Alice and Annie exchanged glances. That's exactly what they had exclaimed when they opened the front door to the old house.

"I drove by there, oh, it must have been around Christmas time on my way Down East to see an old friend in Hancock County," Mary Beth said. "That place just looks awful. I don't know why someone doesn't just tear it down."

"It's sad to see what was once a beautiful old home just go to ruin that way." Gwen put down her work and gazed at nothing.

Annie carefully put her toe in the water of this discussion.

"You remember it then, Gwen? I mean before it became so run down?"

"Oh, sure I do! And you, too, don't you Mary Beth? And Alice?"

The women nodded, but Alice added, "Just barely. I hardly ever go out on Doss Road."

"Well, it *is* off the beaten track," Stella said.

"Do you know anything about it … I mean, the people who owned it … or lived in it?" Annie asked the group in general. "Or even why it's been left empty for so long? I mean, it just seems so sad … ." She let her voice trail because somehow that observation seemed disloyal to Gram.

"Stony Point's Nancy Drew," laughed Peggy. "Trust Annie to want to know the wherefores and the whys."

Stella fixed a sharp gaze on Annie for so long that, Annie fidgeted.

"I think there's more to her interest than she's letting on," the older woman said at last. "And maybe it has something to do with these people she was asking about earlier."

Annie stared at Stella in dismay. Oh, how could she have been so transparent! She should know by now the women of the Hook and Needle Club were sharp-eyed and sharp-witted … and stubborn.

"You might as well tell them," Alice said.

Annie gave her a frown, but Alice waved it off.

"Annie, they are going to find out sooner or later."

"What?" Mary Beth said, her curiosity so keen it was nearly visible. Her reputation for inquisitiveness—some even said she was nosy—was well-earned.

"Yes, for goodness sake!" Kate put in. "Tell us this new secret. Don't make us drag it out of you, word by word."

Six pairs of bright eyes fixed on Annie, eagerly waiting.

"Alice, I swear—," she scolded her friend. She and Alice had already talked about this, and she thought the other woman understood her desire to keep the mystery surrounding Fairview under wraps for a while. Obviously not.

Annie had to admit that her friend had a point. Maybe one of the Hook and Needle Club members could help her learn why Gram owned that old place, and why she had allowed it to fall into such disrepair. She sighed in resignation.

"I found a deed in the cedar chest."

"A deed?" said Kate.

"Not a deed to Foulview, by any chance?" Peggy all but squealed.

"Yes. And please don't call it that. That name makes it sound so … disgusting. The thing is … ." She paused, and then blurted out, "The thing is, that deed is in Gram's name."

A stunned, short silence fell over the group.

"Are you telling us that Elizabeth Holden, my dearest girlhood friend, owned that piece of real estate and simply let it go to rack and ruin?" Stella was all but glaring at Annie.

"I'm sorry, but yes. That's what it looks like."

"Impossible!" Stella announced, as if that one word could put everything right. "Betsy was too conscientious to let that happen."

"Yes, I agree! And well, that's just a part of the mystery. The other part is, who are Joseph and Alta Harper? They owned Fairview before she did and signed it over to her. But who are they? Where are they? Why doesn't anyone remember them? Stony Point is not big enough for people to live here and suddenly go missing, or at least remain totally unknown."

"You have a curiosity there, for sure," Mary Beth said.

"So have you been out there to Fairview and seen the place?" Kate asked, wide-eyed.

"Up close and personal," Alice answered, "and believe me, it was no picnic."

"Maybe not," Annie said stoutly, "but I'm going back. There's something about it that—"

"Stay away from that old house!" Stella said, her voice like the sharp report of a rifle.

~ 8 ~

Everyone looked at Stella in surprise. She had leaned forward, eyes flashing, her gaze pinned on Annie. Usually when the woman spoke, it was quietly, in cultivated tones meant to convey class and decorum. Snapping loudly at anyone seemed unnatural.

"Why, Stella!" Annie said. "Why do you say that?"

"She's right," Mary Beth said. "No one should be snooping around that old place."

Annie drew herself poker straight and looked at the store owner. "Why not? Especially as it seems Fairview is mine now."

"Because it will fall in on your head, you silly girl," Stella said. "Any old building left to itself is going to deteriorate to the point of being a danger."

"If the roof doesn't collapse, the floor might," Mary Beth said, "or that old chimney could give way. There is a multitude of things that could happen."

"Or not," Annie said, a little put out by all the cautionary predictions. "It looked sound enough to me the other day. Just dirty and deserted for far too long."

"Humph!" Peggy said. "Give me an old floor, or an old roof, or an old chimney any day. I do not like ghosts."

"Ghosts?" Annie stared at her. "What do you mean 'ghosts'?"

"You know. Ghosts. People without bodies. Everyone knows Fairview is haunted. That's why no one has set foot in there for so long. In fact, that is probably why the Harpers gave it to Betsy, and why she left it alone and never mentioned it to you."

"Oh, Peggy," Annie laughed, shaking her head.

"You mean, real ghosts?" Kate asked, eyes wide. "With chains and everything?"

"Of course, real ghosts," Peggy said.

"You don't believe that nonsense, surely!" Annie said. She looked from one to the other.

Kate met Annie's disbelieving eyes a moment longer, and then blinked. "No. No, of course not! But it sounds, you know—" She shuddered. "Creepy!"

"Ghosts, my foot!" Stella said, "More like hoboes and tramps."

"Are there such things as hoboes these days?" Alice said, and then wistfully added, "I always thought it would be fun to be a hobo. You know, ride the rails, go from town to town, see new things every day—"

"Eat out of garbage bins and drink from old tin cans? Beg for food, never take a bath? That's your idea of fun?" Mary Beth shook her head. "You have crazy notions, sometimes, Alice."

"Yeah," added Peggy. "If you were a hobo, how would you be able to keep up with your cross-stitch?"

They all broke into laughter at that. Gwen gathered her knitting needles and yarn and put them in her tote.

"This is a fascinating subject," she said, "and I hate to leave you ladies, but I have a dental appointment in Portland. I asked his office staff to schedule me for any day but Tuesday, but wouldn't you know, this is the only day free, unless I wanted to wait until late June. I would prefer to get it over with, thank you very much!"

She gave a little wave as they said their goodbyes and left the meeting.

"Well, I for one do *not* believe in ghosts," Annie said after the door closed behind Gwen, "and I've been inside Fairview. It needs work. A lot of work. But it isn't falling in. I'm not afraid to go back out there, and I plan on doing so. But I also want to find out who the Harpers are, and why Gram owned that place."

"Betsy never told you about it?" Peggy asked. "Not even a hint?"

"Never. Not the least little hint. Alice had to tell me where Fairview was located. And another thing: Gram never mentioned Joseph and Alta Harper, either."

Stella examined her last row of stitches, and then said, "Could be there was a good reason for that." She looked up. "Betsy was not the type to do things for no good reason."

"I agree," Annie told her. "And this is why I've been so reluctant to share this bit of news with you."

Mary Beth narrowed her eyes. "Are you saying you think Betsy did something ... underhanded?"

"Why, no! Of course not. Gram was not that kind of person."

"And yet you have been so secretive about this. You found the deed when?"

"Several days ago."

"Odd to me that you didn't even want to tell your

friends," Stella said, exchanging a glance with Mary Beth.

"Yes. Almost like you don't trust us," Mary Beth said, then added, "Or your grandmother."

"Why, no! That's not true at all. I just wanted to wait a bit, until I knew more."

This line of conversation made Annie uncomfortable, twining confusion, guilt, and defensiveness around her until she wanted to leave the meeting. She looked at Alice who placidly continued to work on her cross-stitch. Annie wished with all her heart her friend had seen fit to keep quiet about the deed for a little longer.

Suddenly all Annie's earlier homesickness sprang up anew. She knew Wayne would have recognized her need to understand this enigmatic side of Gram that was so mysterious. LeeAnn, in her youthful wisdom, would have been able to discuss the facets of this latest bit of knowledge. It seemed no one who surrounded Annie right then had the least inkling of how the discovery of this latest mystery had affected her.

Annie looked at every member of the group, one by one. She wanted to get away from those curious stares and those expressions that seemed almost accusatory in their intent.

Early on, when she had first moved to Stony Point, Annie had not had the easiest time fitting in. Sure, most of the club members had been friendly and welcoming, but some of them—especially Stella—had held her at arm's length, as if she had had any other agenda than wanting to be a part of the circle they'd formed. She thought she had overcome all that. And now … .

She had fought homesickness and loneliness for her

family so much the last few weeks, that her mood had often bordered miserable. Now that she had finally made some progress, was she willing to give any of it up? No way! She was not about to let anyone or anything else defeat her today.

She swallowed hard, straightened her shoulders.

"I am going back out to Doss Road, and I am going to look through Fairview again. Do any of you want to go with me?"

There was the briefest of silences.

"Pfft!" said Mary Beth, flicking one hand. "Not me. That place is dangerous."

"Nor I." Stella knitted energetically, a deep furrow between her brows. "I'm not about to break my neck prowling around some old wreck of a house."

"I might not like them, but I want to look for ghosts." Peggy said emphatically.

"There aren't any ghosts," Annie told her.

Peggy met her eyes. "Listen. You'll probably want to sell Foulview—I mean, Fairview. Believe me when I say that no one will want to buy it if they think it's haunted. Right?"

Annie thought about it. She did not want to keep the place, of course. And she acknowledged very few buyers, if any, would show interest in the house if they believed ghosts ran amuck through the rooms.

"This way, if we go and see or hear any spirits lurking around," Peggy continued with increasing enthusiasm, "we can call in specialists to run them out, or send them on their way, or show them the light, or whatever it is those people do."

"We won't see or hear any spirits—" Annie began.

"But if we do," Peggy interrupted, raising her voice a bit, "we can have them taken care of."

"And if we don't," Alice said, "we can swear the place isn't haunted. It's a win-win situation. Right?"

Annie sighed. "Right. But we aren't going to see any ghosts."

Alice crimped her lips. "Sometimes, Annie, you can be such a buzzkill."

Annie's mouth flew open.

"What in the world is a 'buzzkill'?" Stella asked, looking up.

"Vanessa uses that term more than I like." Kate said. "It means a 'party pooper'."

"I am *not* a party pooper," Annie declared. "Or a buzzkill, or a fuddy-duddy, or any other crazy epithet you wish to hang on me. I'm just realistic."

"Ha!" Alice said, but she was grinning. "OK, then. How many of you would like to go to Fairview on a ghost-chasing expedition?" She raised her right hand.

Peggy's hand shot into the air, and Alice continued to hold up her own.

"Annie?" she said, one eyebrow up. "We are doing this for you."

Annie sighed and slowly raised her hand. "All right. Fine. We'll seek out ghosts."

Kate, Stella and Mary Beth kept their hands busy knitting, crocheting, or in Mary Beth's case, straightening a display on the counter.

"Then it's the three of us," Alice said.

"Yes. But we have to go at night!" Peggy made the absurd pronouncement in a perfectly reasonable tone of voice.

"At night?" Stella and Mary Beth echoed. Annie gaped at her wordlessly.

"Have you lost your mind?" Mary Beth said. "That place has no lights. There aren't even any streetlights that far out of town."

"That's what flashlights are for," Peggy told her.

"Haven't you seen those ghost-hunting guys on television?" Alice added. "They only go hunting at night, and on every single one of those shows, they turn out all the lights before they look for the ghosts."

"Oh, good grief!" Stella barked. "I've never heard such a ridiculous plan in my life. Annie, tell me you have better sense than these two."

Annie looked at her friends, their bright eyes and eager smiles. They were itching for adventure, and she had to admit an adventure was just what she needed, foolish as this one seemed to be. She gave Stella a grin.

"If the pros do it that way, then far be it from me to look for ghosts in the broad light of day."

Stella and Mary Beth exchanged glances.

"Did you ever?" Stella said.

Mary Beth shook her head. "Not in all my days." She looked at the trio and said, "You'd better carry a big stick and some mace."

That sent Annie into such a fit of giggles that Peggy and Alice joined in.

"Oh, goodness, Mary Beth," she managed to gasp. "I can see it now. I will spray the ghost with mace, and while it's screaming in pain, Peggy and Alice can whack it on the head with sticks."

"Just one question, though," Alice said, wheezing. "What'll we do with it once we've got it subdued?"

~ 9 ~

Since Peggy had to work that Tuesday after the Hook and Needle Club meeting, the women agreed to set the ghost quest for Thursday night. For Annie, the whole venture seemed more silly than adventurous.

"Mom, you have always been so down to earth and responsible," LeeAnn said when Annie called her Tuesday night. "Sometimes you need a little silly in your life. It will help to keep you young."

"Young? Maybe so, but it seems to me more like a trek into a second childhood," Annie said dryly. "I mean, really. Ghosts? And in the dark of night? Peggy said it's easier to see shadows and movement in the dark. Now, I don't understand that logic at all. Plus, she said it being dark and all will help us focus. I think that tactic will help us be so focused on seeing something that we probably will, whether anything is there or not! "

LeeAnn laughed.

"Now, Mom," she chided, "keep an open mind. That's what you have always told me, isn't it? And anyway, like you said, if you can disprove rumors that the place is haunted, then you're more apt to sell it."

Annie sighed. "As if anyone wants it, anyway. Honey, it needs so much work, and I'm just not sure I want to tackle it."

"Then sell it, as is. Let the new owners worry about fixing it up."

"Believe me, LeeAnn, I've considered that. But, I just don't know … ."

"Well, think about it some more, will you? You never know when someone is looking for a bargain."

"That's true. Especially these days. Although, I have to say I sincerely doubt Fairview will turn out to be a bargain for anyone."

LeeAnn gave a soft, quick laugh. "Let's hope you're wrong, Mom. Have you had any word about the folks who gave it to Gram?"

"I talked with Mike Malone at the hardware store, and he is going to go through some of his records for me. He's a pretty good historian, so we'll see what he finds."

"That's great, Mom," LeeAnn said. "Be sure to let me know what you learn, OK? And whatever you do, relax and have some fun."

That night, with LeeAnn's suggestions and support blanketing her worries, Annie was able to snuggle down in her bed and sleep well for the first time in several nights.

* * *

"You're not wearing *that*, are you?" Alice asked when Annie opened the front door to her Thursday evening.

Annie glanced down at her faded jeans and a star-spangled, red, white, and blue hoody sweatshirt with the words "Lone Star State" stenciled across the back.

"This seems appropriate for the occasion," Annie said

with a puzzled smile. "What should I wear, Donna Karan or Calvin Klein?"

Alice snorted, and stepped through the door.

"Ha, ha. You're too funny. Actually, what you should wear is something dark so you'll blend into the shadows."

"Oh, for heaven's sake!" Annie sputtered. "'Blend into the shadows,' indeed. Why? So the ghosts won't see me?"

Alice grimaced. "Will you be serious?"

"Well, it's a little hard to be serious when there is a dress code for ghost chasing."

Alice huffed. Her glance dropped to Annie's feet.

"Annie Dawson, you are not wearing those sneakers out to Fairview."

Annie drew herself up, started to protest, but Alice spoke over her.

"Have you already forgotten how muddy that yard was when we were there the other day? Just because we haven't had rain in the last twenty-four hours doesn't mean there is dry ground out there. You need to wear something sturdy."

"Oh. Well, that's the first thing you've said tonight that makes sense. And don't stick your tongue out at me. That's very unattractive. I'll change my shoes, but I thought we had a good chance of snow tonight."

"I heard that too," Alice said. "And it is quite windy outside. The ground is cold, but it isn't frozen."

"Well, as I said before, I'll put on different shoes, but I am not changing clothes," Annie declared. Before her friend had an opportunity to suggest they fashion and wear hats made of aluminum foil, she added, "I have a pair of brogans in the closet that has seen a good deal of mud in my garden in

Texas. They should be more than sturdy enough for Fairview. If you want some hot chocolate, I have some on the stove. Help yourself. I'll be right back."

A few minutes later, Annie clomped back downstairs in her heavy, ankle-high work boots. Alice was sitting cross-legged on the living room floor, a mug of hot chocolate in one hand and stroking Boots from head to tail with the other. The cat arched her back and Annie could hear her purring all the way across the room.

"Boots loves that attention," Annie said. "In fact, she can be a regular little pig about it sometimes."

Alice looked up and smiled. "She's a sweet kitty. Listen to her purr! And I'd swear that she's smiling."

They looked at the relaxed gray cat who lay, basking and contented, beneath Alice's stroking fingers.

"By the way," Alice said, "I like how you arranged those baskets in the corner. Very chic."

"Coming from a Divine Décor representative, that's high praise."

"Did you find them in the attic?"

Annie nodded. "Where else? They were tucked back in a corner, and I thought they would make a great place to keep the rest of my yarn and thread."

"Good thinking," Alice agreed. She glanced around. "But I thought you were using the cedar chest. What did you do with it?"

"Oh, I am using it, for sure, but it didn't hold half of that yarn. The chest is in the library. That lovely old wood needed to be in a place where there are books and a comfy leather chair. Plus, I love to sit in the window seat and crochet. The view from there is just so lovely."

"Yes," Alice sighed. "It is. You are lucky to have so many gorgeous views here at Grey Gables."

"Yes, I am. But you have good views from your house."

"I do! But not from every window the way you do. The builder of this old house was a wise architect."

The doorbell rang.

"That will be Peggy. Excuse me, Alice, while I let her in." She went to open the door.

"Greetings, earthlings," Peggy said, grinning, wiggling her eyebrows. She was dressed in ratty jeans, denim coat and ancient scuffed boots. "Are you ready for our adventure?"

She stepped inside, the black strap of a bulging backpack over one shoulder.

"What in the world do you have there?" Annie asked. She and Alice eyed the black-and-white pack as Peggy tugged it off.

"I think Wally said he used this thing in high school," she told them.

She unbuckled the straps, opened it, pulled out the contents and spread them on the living-room floor for their perusal: assorted flashlights, two packs of batteries, two small tape recorders, a package of mini-cassettes, a cell phone, a digital camera, candles, matches, air freshener, a bag of chips, an assortment of candy bars, and a VHS cassette.

All three women stood and stared at the motley heap on the floor in front of them, and Annie finally raised her eyes, mystified.

"What's all that for?"

Peggy gaped at her. "Are you kidding? This is our equipment."

"Equipment for what?"

"Annie! Where is your mind? This is our ghost-hunting equipment, of course! And if you have a digital camera, go get it. I only have this one."

"You need Almond Joys to look for ghosts?" Annie said. "You expect to run into one with a sweet tooth?"

"Will you be serious? I brought the candy bars for us, in case we get hungry in the middle of the night—"

"Middle of the night!" Annie squawked. "And air freshener? Honestly, Peggy, why did you—"

Peggy glowered. "If we're going to do this, we have to do it right."

"But I do not want to spend the night in that old house. It's dirty and cold—"

Standing next to her, Alice gave Annie a surreptitious little nudge. Annie glanced at her friend, then shot a sharp look at Peggy. Both women stared back, Alice with patience and curiosity, Peggy with her hands on her hips and defiance in her eyes.

Annie knew Peggy worked long, hard hours at the diner to help keep her household going. Her husband, Wally, worked hard too, building, repairing, doing whatever anyone needed him to do, but the economy was not kind to blue-collar workers these days, and the Carson family struggled. Wally and Peggy devoted themselves to raising their little girl, and it was obvious that they were excellent parents, but Annie knew from experience that child-rearing was never easy, even in the best of circumstances when money and resources were plentiful. How much more difficult it must be to work hard day after day and still come up short repeatedly! It must be so discouraging.

At that moment Annie finally realized how much this little adventure meant to the younger woman. It was a break for Peggy, a virtual escape, from the routine and duty, just for an evening.

She scolded herself for not realizing it earlier.

"Maybe I should throw together some sandwiches to go with those candy bars?" Annie said by way of making amends.

The tension drained from Peggy's face.

"Well, maybe a Thermos of coffee?" she suggested with a smile.

"Sure! I'll go make some fresh right now."

She started to walk away but paused when Alice said, "Peggy, why do you have that videotape?"

"That's our training video, of course. You have a VCR don't you, Annie?"

"I didn't think anyone watched video tapes these days," Alice said. "Do they even make VCRs anymore?"

Peggy shrugged. "A VCR is all we have right now. It might be old, but it still works really well." She picked up the tape and waved it around. "This is a recording of one of those paranormal investigation shows I was telling you about earlier. We will watch the experts before we leave so we'll know what to do tonight."

Annie coughed discreetly and tried not to grimace. She had never liked anything that smacked of magic and superstition.

"I have a VCR, and it still works. If you want to turn on the TV and get the tape ready, Peggy, I'll go make that coffee and then join you."

"This seems to be turning into a regular party," Alice

said. "I should have baked cookies and brought chips and dip."

"Maybe," said Annie with a bright smile she did not feel, "if we finish up, uh, earlier than expected, we can come back here for those sandwiches."

Peggy said, with emphasis, "Breakfast sandwiches."

"All right. Breakfast sandwiches, then."

In her head, Annie added, *How did they ever talk me into this crazy adventure?*

When she came back into the room after making coffee, Peggy and Alice had settled on the floor cross-legged, in front of the television, like two little girls on Saturday morning. The TV screen presented a static image of a serious-looking man, and his shorter, younger sidekick. They appeared frozen in the middle of a conversation.

"Coffee's going," she told the pair, "and a Thermos is at the ready."

"Okay, Annie. Come here and watch this with us." Peggy patted a patch of floor next to her. "It has just started, so I paused the tape for you, but be sure to pay attention."

She pointed the remote control at the stack of media machines below Annie's flatscreen television, pushed the pause button, and the two men jumped to life.

"… so she believes an entity lives in the music room?" the older man was asking the younger.

"That seems to be where most of the activity takes place in the house," the other man replied. "They say they've been hearing noises all over the house, including a voice that calls a name. Plus, they have heard strange knocking sounds in the bedroom at odd hours during the day."

Annie's doorbell rang right then, and all three women jumped an inch, at least. They looked at each other, and Alice said, "Are you expecting company, Annie?"

"Just you two, but in Stony Point, friends often drop in without calling from time to time. I better see who is on the other side of my door."

When she opened the front door, Annie saw Kate Stevens, dark-hair pulled back, eyes wide, face a white oval in the soft glow of the porch light.

"Well, Kate! What a surprise! Come on in."

Kate stepped across the threshold, hands buried deep in the pocket of her heavy wool peacoat.

"Kate!" Alice hollered from her spot on the floor.

"Hiya, Kate," Peggy said, rewinding the tape. "You coming with us?"

Annie recalled the uneasiness Kate displayed at the mere mention of Fairview's haunted reputation. *Of course she's not coming with us*, she thought.

"Yes," Kate said, her voice shaking slightly. She cleared her throat and stated firmly, "Yes. I am."

～ 10 ～

Annie's mouth dropped open. *"You're going?"* she said finally to Kate.

"Yes," the woman said firmly. "I want some adventure in my life."

By this time Peggy and Alice stood on either side of Annie, facing Kate. Annie was sure their expressions of astonishment mirrored her own. Peggy, though, was also grinning like a monkey.

"Come inside, Kate." Annie stepped aside as her friend came into the house.

She closed the door against the invasion of cold wind. All four women stood in a cluster a few feet from the front door.

"What changed your mind?" Annie asked.

The woman drew up her shoulders, took a deep breath and let it out.

"I've been through some hard times lately, you know," Kate said. She looked at each friend in turn. "And I hate to admit it, but I have allowed circumstances to get me down these last few months. Keeping life at home as close to normal as possible, and tending to Vanessa, making sure she's all right, has been … well, it's been more than a little difficult, as you know. I am so tired of being on edge, and feeling uncertain and let down."

She looked away, her cheeks pink as if she was embarrassed to admit feeling all too human. When her gaze returned to the three women, her face registered hard-won determination.

"I decided I want some adventure in my life," she announced. "Even if it scares the living daylights out of me."

There was just the briefest silence, and then Annie slipped her arm around Kate's straight, but shaking shoulder and drew her further into the room.

"We are happy and proud to have you come along on this … little adventure."

"I even came prepared," Kate said, pulling her hands from her pockets. In her left hand she held a flashlight, and in the right she held a small recorder and a digital camera. "Just like the guys on that TV show."

* * *

Later, after the four women watched and discussed the program Peggy had recorded, they gathered their supplies, including the coffee, disposable cups and candy bars.

"Peggy," Annie said, "I'm still curious about the air freshener. Those people on television didn't use it—not even one time. So why are we talking it with us?"

Peggy's expression said Annie just didn't "get it."

"Annie. Any house that has been closed up for years and years, especially out in the middle of nowhere, is going to have an unpleasant odor. In fact, closed-up houses stink."

"Febreze has absolutely nothing to do with the supernatural," Alice chimed in, "and everything in the world to do with eradicating stinky air."

Annie felt foolish, and a little bit chastised. "Oh. Okay, then," she said humbly. "That makes sense."

With their arms as full as if they were going on a weekend camping trip, the women piled into Annie's Malibu and headed toward Fairview. Alice and Peggy chattered madly in the backseat. Kate sat silent and clench-fisted in the front passenger seat while Annie guided the car along the highway to Doss Road. At last she turned the car onto the rutted, muddy lane that led to the house. The car's headlights washed over the trees and overgrown shrubs and threw the yard into deep shadows.

The women got out of the car, and stood a moment, staring at their destination.

"It does look eerie, doesn't it?" Alice said in an undertone. "Especially at night."

"But don't you think most places look a little eerie at night?" Annie asked.

"Annie is one hundred percent right," Peggy stated. "Come on, ladies! Onward and forward."

The quartet gingerly picked their way across the gummy yard toward the house. The weathered siding seemed to absorb all brightness from their flashlights without allowing any illumination to spread. The closer they got, the more the old house took on a deeper, almost sinister aura in the murky darkness.

The other three huddled behind Annie as she fumbled with the old key and lock. They stood so close she could almost feel them breathing down her neck.

"It will probably take all of us to push this thing open,"

she said, but at that moment the key turned with her first attempt, and the door swung open.

"Oh, my," Annie said, faintly.

"That was easier than the other day," Alice told her. "I still have a bruise on my shoulder."

Annie opened her mouth to say she had not even so much as turned the knob, let alone pushed against the door itself, but one glance at Kate's nervous face kept her silent. She admired the other woman's spunk, but it seemed to Annie that something deeper than just a little hesitation to explore the old house lay within Kate's fear. Perhaps Kate's answer to this night's adventure call was the way to fill an emptiness created by the years she had spent locked in an unhappy marriage. At least she was out of that relationship now, but the aftereffects often lingered for years. If exploring a dank old house at night was part of Kate's do-it-yourself therapy, Annie questioned the wisdom of including the younger woman in this mad errand. In fact, seeing a professional counselor seemed more prudent.

Peggy eagerly stepped over the threshold, and Alice followed. They stood for a moment just beyond the doorway, skimming the interior with the beams from their flashlights. Peggy ventured farther into the dark room.

"Are you all right, Kate?" Annie murmured, lingering on the porch with her uneasy friend. "Do you want to wait in the car, or would you like to go back home? It's okay, if you do. We'll all understand."

Kate moved restlessly, took in a deep breath, squared her shoulders and met Annie's gaze in the leftover light.

"Thanks, Annie, but I'm fine. Just because I saw a ghost

once before doesn't mean I can't take seeing another one. The whole experience was probably all in my imagination, anyway."

"What?" Alice said, swinging her flashlight around to assault Kate's face. "What did you say, Kate?"

Kate drew back, squinted and turned her head to fend off the light. "Please!" she exclaimed. "Get that out of my eyes, or all I'll see from now until next Christmas is a bright blue splotch!"

"Oh. Sorry." Alice lowered the flashlight. "Did you say you've seen a ghost?"

Kate sighed. "I thought I did. But it was a long time ago, and I ... well, never mind."

Peggy came trotting back to the door. "Oo! Do tell!"

"Not now," Kate said. "Let's see what Fairview has to offer." She resolutely stepped past Peggy, leading Annie into the house. She glanced around at the darkened corners. "And I think we should shut the door."

"Oh, I thought I would run out to the car and turn on the lights to shine inside, to help us see better," Annie suggested.

"Oh, Annie!" Peggy said in disgust. "Didn't you learn anything from that video tonight? Haven't you paid attention to *anything* I told you?"

"The thing is, Annie," Kate said, as if explaining a simple crochet pattern, "if you're hoping actually to see something, you really need it as dark as possible in here. Spirits often manifest as nothing more than shadows or flickers of energy. When the light shines, the shadows you see might be made from objects in the room. Plus, outside noises will contaminate sounds we hear inside, so it's better to have doors and windows closed."

Annie listened to these statements with considerable amazement.

"Where'd you come up with all that?" she asked.

"Who cares?" Peggy said. "It makes sense."

"Well, if *I* hear a noise, I'm turning on my flashlight to see if it's a mouse," Alice said stoutly. "I don't mind seeing a ghost, but I do *not* want to see a mouse."

"No!" Peggy said. "Alice MacFarlane, don't you dare turn on your flashlight!"

"If you do that, you will ruin everything," Kate said.

"But those people on the show turned on their flashlights sometimes," Annie said. "And they had camera lights. How else could they film the program?"

"Those are special lights that they use," Peggy said shortly.

"I am not going to stand here and let a mouse run up my pants leg!" Alice's voice went up an octave or two as she spoke.

"Just do us a favor, then," Peggy snapped. "Go wait in the car."

Annie disliked the ugly turn the evening suddenly seemed to be taking. The bad atmosphere that was brewing inside Fairview just underscored the whole miserable aspect of the old house, and she found it all disturbing. She heartily wished she and her friends had never embarked on this scheme.

"Ladies," she said, "maybe we ought to just—"

"Peggy Carson!" Alice all but yelled, "I most certainly will not wait in the car! I have as much right to be here as you do, and I want to—"

"Stop it!" Kate shouted, sounding like a drill sergeant. In the glow of four flashlights, she glowered at the two bickering women who stared at her with wide eyes. "Now, you listen to me. If you hear something, just be very quiet. We'll be able to tell if it's a mouse or not." Kate became the quiet voice of reason and strength. "If it's a mouse, I'll take care of it."

The other women continued to gape at her. Where had her timidity gone?

"So where do we start?" Annie said, dragging her gaze off Kate to settle on Peggy.

Peggy handed her flashlight to Alice and dug into her backpack. She pulled out her tape player.

"Kate, do you have your recorder?"

Kate pulled it out of her coat pocket.

"Good. I wish we had more than two of them," Peggy said. "You saw on the program that most of the proof of paranormal entities was found on the recorders."

"But weren't the ones they used those high-end, techno-sophisticated digital recorders?" Annie asked.

"But these are what we have, so they will just have to do."

"And didn't they also have those special cameras that see in the dark and measure heat and—"

"Annie, for Pete's sake, do you have to be such a Debbie downer?" Alice said.

"Is that the same thing as a buzzkill?"

"Yes, it surely is! And this isn't like you. Where is your sense of adventure, anyway?"

Annie cringed inwardly. She truly was not trying to ruin this adventure for the others. The whole ghost-chasing bit seemed so far-fetched, and she was usually so practical, that it was hard to see past all the nonsense. Recalling her earlier conversation with LeeAnn, and how her daughter had encouraged Annie to keep an open mind and have fun, she resolved to stuff that practical self into the background for the night.

"Okay, then," Annie said brightly. She gripped her flashlight tightly and grinned. "Let's do it."

"And let's have no more nonsense from anyone," Peggy said. She paused to let this sink into the other three brains. "We really should break up into teams of two," she continued. "Since Annie and Alice have been here before, they will be leaders. I'll go with Alice, and Kate, you go with Annie. You two start with that room right over there."

She pointed the flashlight at the bedroom door on the far side of the living room. That was the room where Annie and Alice had heard noises, and where Annie had actually seen something move. She pondered telling Kate, but not wanting to resurrect the woman's anxiety she choose to keep silent about it.

Annie took a deep breath, and with a zest she did not feel, said, "C'mon, Kate. Let's go bust us some ghosts. Be careful you don't bark your shins on this furniture in the dark."

"Lead on," Kate said enthusiastically. "I'm right behind you!"

They wended their way carefully toward the bedroom.

"Be sure to take pictures." Peggy called after them, adding, "And do not forget to turn off those flashlights!" She and Alice were already heading down the black-as-night hallway. At least in the dark Peggy couldn't see Annie roll her eyes.

Annie pushed open the door, wincing as its hinges screeched like every door of every haunted house in every cheesy horror flick ever made. It was as awful as fingernails scraping down a blackboard. She sensed, rather than saw or felt, Kate shudder behind her.

Alice and Peggy could—and probably would—set up a howling protest, but Annie refused to turn off her flashlight and plunge them into murky darkness before taking a moment to look around the room. She would rather not run into the wall or stub her toe on a piece of furniture.

The bedroom lay in dusty, dim relief as they flushed the interior with their light beams. Annie stepped inside and Kate followed.

"What a lovely room," Kate said, as if they were standing in a four-star hotel on a sunny day. "Look at that painting!" She crossed the room, directing her flashlight across the face of an impressionistic painting. She touched it. "Feel that texture," she said. "Even under all that dust, it's obvious that this is an original. Oh, I'd love to see it in the daylight!"

After a bit she threw the beam around the room while Annie focused her light on the corner that had mystified and frightened her and Alice the other day.

"Did you see this coverlet?" Kate asked. "Such a gorgeous pattern."

Annie looked over her shoulder, saw Kate bent over the bed, studying the cross-stitch work.

"Yes, I saw it the day Alice and I were out here. It's lovely. In fact, there are quite a few lovely things in this house.

"You should take these things home, Annie, and have them cleaned. The painting, the coverlet, those darling little pillows in that old rocker over there."

"Kate … ?"

The other woman lifted her head, looked at Annie, smiling. "Yes?"

Annie stared at her, still astounded by the transformation from the apprehensive woman on her doorstep earlier in the evening to the casual, confident woman in front of her at that moment. Maybe all it took was purpose and a need to bring about change. Maybe Kate's do-it-yourself therapy was a good idea, after all.

"What is it you wanted to say, Annie?" Kate prodded.

Annie shook her head. "Nothing. Just … are you having a good time?"

"Yes. Except for the squabble between those two in there."

They shared a smile.

"I'm glad," Annie said.

Kate laughed.

"Me too," she said. "But we are here to look for spirits, not handiwork, aren't we?"

"Unfortunately, yes." Annie let out a sigh of resignation.

"I just got caught up in this lovely old place," Kate said. "I had no idea Foulview could be so marvelously surprising." She turned the light to her tape recorder, adding, "Annie, why don't you take some pictures."

"Of what? Nothing will show up, we don't have enough light."

"The flash ought to brighten the areas you snap. Turn off your flashlight and just take random pictures. Remember what those guys did on Peggy's video." She fiddled with the tape recorder, lifted her head, and to no one Annie could see, Kate casually said, "Is anyone in here with us?"

"Kate, do you really expect someone to answer?"

"Won't know until we try, will we?"

Kate turned off the flashlight. After a moment's hesitation, Annie turned off hers, too.

"Hello? My name is Kate. The lady with me is my friend, Annie. Can you tell us your name, please?"

A long, unbroken silence followed. In spite of her strong skepticism, Annie knew if some unearthly voice replied, she would probably faint dead away.

"Annie," Kate whispered, "take the pictures."

Without a word but feeling incredibly foolish, Annie picked up her camera, turned it on, pointed it in various spots in the room and pressed the button—flash after flash—until she was sure she had blinded every specter hovering around.

After a bit, Kate moved and said, "Let's go into another room."

Annie started to leave but stopped. Maybe she was getting into the swing of things, or maybe she was just being silly, but she could not leave the room without another look at that mysterious corner.

"Wait a minute, Kate. Would you please come over here to this corner?"

"Did you see something?" Kate whispered as she approached.

"Not tonight, but the other day ..." she whispered back. "I'm not sure. It was dark in here. Not as dark as right now, but you know, gray and dim. And this corner ...."

Kate said aloud, "Is someone in this corner?"

The pair stood still, breathless and wide-eyed, waiting. Perhaps there was the sound of slight movement. Maybe it was her imagination. Annie lifted the camera and fired off several flashes from all angles. There was a definite noise, louder this time, like the scattering of rocks. Kate gasped, and Annie reached out for her. They grabbed each other's hands, not moving, but watching, straining to see in the darkness. The sound of knocking, a loud thump so near it seemed they could touch it had they not been frozen in place.

Annie stifled a scream, and Kate drew in a shuddering breath.

"Who's here?" she said, her voice quivering. To Annie, frantically, "Take pictures, take pictures!"

Annie snapped photos of the corner as fast as her camera could process the action.

A loud scream from another part of the house and both women jumped so hard they bumped into each other. Annie's camera nearly slipped from her shaking fingers as she and Kate raced across the room.

"What happened?" Annie cried as they burst into the living room the same time Alice and Peggy charged from the back of the house. All four flashlights blazed, lighting the room.

"What happened?" Annie asked again.

"Didn't you guys hear that?" Alice said. "Don't tell me you didn't hear it!"

"Oh, my word! It was awful!" Peggy gasped, one fist pressed to her chest as if to slow down her heartbeat.

"You both heard all that knocking and thumping?" asked

Annie. "We thought it was just in the bedroom."

"Knocking and thumping? Are you kidding? No!" Peggy nearly shouted. "It was a shriek. Like someone in pain."

"And then cold air all around us," Alice added. "Just like the other day when we were here, Annie, only worse."

Kate gaped at them. "You heard someone scream?"

"Yes! Didn't you?" Peggy looked from Kate's face to Annie's, and back to Kate's.

"And that cold air that went across us!" Alice added, shuddering. "It was like an icy breath."

"Did you see *The Sixth Sense*?" Peggy said. "Whenever ghosts were present, everything got so cold you could see everyone's breath. It was like that."

The quartet stood shivering in the middle of the dusty room. Their flashlights offered a poor substitute for the comforting bright light the women craved. Just then a mournful call wailed out and a blast of cold air enveloped all four women. The cry died, only to come again, louder and longer the second time. Every woman in the room screamed and ran to one another, closing the small space between them, as if to draw strength and protection.

The racket Kate and Annie heard in the bedroom now came again. This time it was above their heads, seeming to be coming from the attic, banging and thumping, then a sound of dragging and glass breaking. The shrieking moan happened again, and the air grew even colder.

"I'm getting out of here!" Peggy shouted. "This is not fun anymore!"

"I'm right behind you," Alice said, following her to the front door.

Peggy grabbed the doorknob. "It won't open!"

"What do you mean, it won't open?" Alice yelled. "Pull it, don't push it! Here, get out of the way. Let me!"

Alice yanked. The door yielded, and they both tumbled backward. When the shriek sounded again, louder than ever, both women screamed like little girls and dashed out into the yard. They seemed to have forgotten their purpose in visiting the old house at night. A bit later they approached the house again, one hesitant, cautious step at a time. They huddled together on the edge of the porch, trying to peer inside the open doorway from that safe distance.

"Annie! Kate!" Peggy called. "Get out of there. Can't you tell whatever is in there doesn't want us around?"

Even though she gave little credence to supernatural events, Annie could barely move her rubbery legs. On the other hand, Kate stayed rooted to the spot. Annie started to move toward the open door.

"Wait a minute, Annie," she said in a low voice, holding out one hand, fingers splayed. "Feel that? The cold breeze is gone."

Annie paused, took note of the air around them.

"You're right. It's gone now."

Kate scoured every wall of the room with her light beam, leaning forward, peering intently.

"And," Annie added, "that awful moaning has hushed."

Kate glanced at her. "When the door opened, it all stopped."

Annie stood in place, looking and listening as carefully as if she were at a train crossing.

"Kate," she said after a moment, "there is not a blessed thing paranormal about that."

"You two girls, get out of the house!" Alice hissed through the open doorway.

"Not yet," Annie told her. "Kate is onto something."

She joined her light to Kate's, and they both tracked the beams along the far wall. Annie looked at her friend, and Kate met her eyes. They shared a smile and walked across the room together, straight toward one of the fearsome ghosts of Fairview.

~ 44 ~

"Annie! Kate! Get out of there!" Peggy shouted. "Fairview is not like those places on the TV shows. C'mon. *Get out.*"

"Peggy, please!" Kate said. "Quit yelling."

"Whatever are you doing in there?" Alice hollered.

Annie did her best to ignore the fretting voices of the less intrepid of the Fairview Ghost Stalkers, but the two women outside continued to plead. Turning a deaf ear proved to be difficult. Annie wanted to cover both her ears with her hands. Instead, she trained her beam on the large stone fireplace that had been built at the midpoint of the wall. Her gaze followed the light as it exposed the layers of dust coating the stones of the chimney. Cobwebs draped like downy ropes from crumbling mortar joints. One of webs swung out in a gentle arc and then swayed in the air as another cold breeze flushed over the two women.

Annie slowly sought with her hand until she found the draft that blew chill air across her fingers.

"There!" she said to Kate. "Right there about six inches above our heads. And look! It's big enough you can slip your hand right in there."

With their two flashlights focused, the gaping hole in the old fireplace seemed to leap into view. As the wind gusted outside, so did the cold breeze through the hole.

"Girls," Annie called to Alice and Peggy. "Come here."

"Is this a trick?"

She wasn't sure which one of her chickenhearted friends on the porch asked that.

"Come in here if you want to find out why you got so cold. And I promise there is not one thing paranormal about it."

A few seconds ticked by. Then, one behind the other and holding hands, Peggy and Alice shuffled into the house. Annie forced herself not to laugh out loud at their cowardly sideways approach.

"What is it?" they asked at the same time.

Outside the wind picked up, hammering itself against the house, shoving through the crack to trail its icy fingers along their faces.

"Oo!" Peggy squealed, taking a step back.

"Stop that!" Kate snapped. "I'm ashamed and surprised at the both of you. You two are the ones who were so determined to go on this ghost investigation, but let a little wind slip through the cracks, and both of you are out the door in a shot."

"Wind through the cracks?" Alice echoed faintly.

"Yes," Annie said. "Come here." She focused her light on the opening.

The pair drew near with as much wariness as they would if they were approaching an autopsy table.

"Come closer," Annie encouraged. "Put your hand right here."

Alice slowly lifted one hand and held it up next to Annie's. Peggy did the same.

"It's damp and cold, just like … ." Peggy bit her lower lip. She shot a glance at her cohort.

Alice, swaying slightly back and forth on the balls of her feet, avoided all eyes by staring at a spot on the dark, dirty ceiling.

"Damp and cold ..." she said, her voice quivering. She took in a deep breath and added, in a squeak, "... as a ghost."

Annie looked at her friend closely. Was the woman about to breakdown? Oh, why had they chosen to embark on this foolish, foolish enterprise! Alice might never forgive her.

Alice's shoulders began to shake. She closed her eyes, clamped her mouth shut so tightly that her lips formed a hard, thin line. Then she bowed her head, and air hissed from her lips, sounding like the release valve on a pressure cooker. To Annie's astonishment, laughter shrieked loose as if held captive too long in the depths of her lungs.

Peggy's mouth flew open as she gawked at her friend. Alice bent double, laughing hysterically. The other three exchanged looks. Peggy's face crumpled.

"I know!" she exclaimed. "A damp, cold ghost!"

A moment later Peggy had clapped both hands over her mouth, gasping as she guffawed like a maniac.

The two women pointed at each other, cackling, stomping, and finally fell weakly against other as they fought to gain control.

"Quivering m-masses of j-jelly"! Alice gasped.

"Yes! Quivering. Jelly. Masses of it," Peggy said. She took a deep, fortifying breath. "I can't believe we just did that. Galumphing that way, right out the front door and into the night."

"Galumphing?" Kate echoed, snickering.

"Stampeding is the better term, I think," Annie told them drily, but giggling all the same.

"But, Annie!" Alice shrieked. "Can quivering jelly stampede?" Her question sent the gutless duo into fits of laughter again. Kate and Annie stood grinning helplessly at them.

As if refusing to be outdone by women, the wind shifted, howled, and rushed around them. The front door slammed shut, startling all four and abruptly halting their merriment. Almost immediately a mournful cry shivered through the dark room. The hair on the back of Annie's neck prickled. The wailing died, but only slightly before building to a crescendo that caused Annie to yearn for escape. She refused to cover her ears and run outside, but she wanted to. Very much.

"I know what that is!" Peggy declared, yelling. "These old windows aren't sealed, I bet."

"I'm sure they aren't," Annie agreed. "They are old— probably original to the house. Some of them are cracked. That horrendous shriek is the wind whistling around them."

"Bet my bottom dollar it is," Peggy said, "and I'm not a betting woman."

"Isn't it awful?" Kate said. "Almost turns *me* into quivering jelly."

Each woman went to a different window and shone their flashlights across the windowsills and cracked panes. At last, they tracked down the alarming doleful cries that had so terrified not only Peggy and Alice, but years of trespassers and adventure-seekers. One shriek came from the kitchen window above the old farm sink, and another came from the window in the first bathroom.

"Now do you wonder why no one else has ever figured

out something so simple?" Annie said, her fists on her hips.

"Because," Kate told her, "they were probably too busy running out the door, squealing like little girls."

They shared another snicker or two at Alice's and Peggy's expense, but Annie had one more observation.

"Well, I am more than happy to disprove all this haunted-house nonsense. In fact, I am thoroughly relieved. But I wonder … you remember all those footsteps and breaking glass we heard in the bedroom, Kate? Something else caused that, because I sincerely doubt any of that was wind coming through gaps around the windows or the fireplace."

Peggy's eyes rounded. "What are you talking about? What exactly did you two hear?"

"Just what Annie said," Kate told her. "Knocks and thumps."

"And glass breaking," Annie added, hoping Peggy would not flee again.

"Yes. Breaking glass."

"Except for the sound of that glass, that is more or less what you and I heard the other day, isn't it, Annie?" Alice asked. She looked to be about half sick. "I think you have … *ick!* … *mice.*"

She shuddered, but Annie was gratified to see her good friend did not hightail it out the door. Annie decided not to mention the shadow she had seen that day. For now, it was good that her two normally down-to-earth friends seemed to have regained most of their wits.

"Let's go have a look," Peggy said, back to her old self. "Annie, you lead the way."

They trailed her like ducklings following their mother. With four flashlights blazing on it, the corner seemed bright as day. Peggy reached out, rapped on the wall, paused, rapped again. Silence greeted them. She looked closely, up and down, examining from floor to ceiling. Then she pressed her cheek close to the wall, shone her light behind the old highboy nearest the corner and tried to see if anything was there. She squatted and continued to peer behind the dusty bureau.

"Aha," she said finally.

"Aha?" Annie and Alice echoed.

"What?" Kate said. "What's back there?"

"You've had visitors," Peggy said at last, getting up and brushing the dust and cobwebs from her head and arm.

"Hoboes?" Alice asked hopefully.

Peggy trained a baleful look on her and shook her head as if Alice was a pesky child.

"No. What is it with you and this newly discovered fascination with transients, anyway?" She turned to Annie. "You've had, and probably still have, rodents."

Alice gave a little shriek. "Rodents?"

"Big rodents."

"Rats?" Alice moaned weakly.

"Undoubtedly. Maybe something else, something bigger."

"*Ewww!*" Alice shuddered as if shaking off something disgusting. Annie was proud that her neighbor stayed in the room with them.

"I think you ought to get my Wally out here to look into this," Peggy continued. "He's a great one to prowl around, find out what is coming in from where. He can fix it so they will not crawl, creep or slide in here again."

Annie smiled at her. Another opportunity to help the Carsons!

"I'm sure he can. And I'll call him, for sure! Thanks, Peggy."

The wind gave an extra exuberant howl about then, and for the first time they could hear the first telltale skittering against the windowpanes.

Annie went to the window, cupped her hands around her eyes and peered outside.

"We have precipitation coming down, ladies. The frozen kind that the weather forecaster on television promised this morning. Maybe we should get home. I still have that Thermos of coffee. If you would like to hang out at Grey Gables for a while, I will fix more hot chocolate and those sandwiches I promised earlier."

"I think that's a good idea," Peggy said. "Everyone, please put your equipment in my bag, and we'll head back to town."

"Peggy," Kate said as they all walked back into the living room. "I think you ought to be on that ghost-hunting show. You're a natural."

~ 12 ~

Saturday morning dawned as lovely and sunny a day as Annie could have asked for. It was rather cold outside, but she loved being outdoors. She sat in the old wicker rocker on the front porch, a crocheted red-and-black plaid afghan around her and Boots curled into a warm, snoozing ball in her lap. On the little table next to her, her cordless phone lay silent but available in case LeeAnn or anyone else called.

Annie sipped from a large mug of hot chocolate and watched the restless movement of the ocean. Sunlight poured unobstructed from the azure blue sky and winked off a couple of lobster boats that bobbed along the undulating water. She watched them for a while, enjoying the cool breeze and the briny smells from the ocean.

After a bit, she set the empty mug on the little table, and plucked out the nearly finished table runner from her crochet tote. She straightened the thread to be sure no kinks or knots could form, and then examined the runner with a critical eye. She only needed to crochet the scalloped edge that framed the whole piece and gave it a sophisticated finish. She thought of edging as a final flourish, something like what a touch of mascara adds to a pair of lovely eyes.

She worked a couple stitches, and Boots popped open one curious eye as she heard the soft whisper of Annie's crocheting. The cat gazed at the thread as it moved from ball, across hook and into a scallop. Boots awakened fully, lifted her head, and lazily batted the thread with one soft, white paw.

"No, no," Annie said, softly. "Mustn't touch."

Boots, of course, had heard this before, and as always, completely ignored the directive. She swatted with more interest, energy, and purpose, and then she stretched her neck and bit the thread.

Annie stopped to gently remove the thin strand from between Boots' sharp teeth. The cat pawed her, claws retracted, and gave her a baleful look.

"If you insist on this, Miss Boots, you will find yourself without a warm lap on which to nap."

Boots blinked, silently meowed as if mouthing, "Please?"

"That argument never works," Annie reminded her.

She crocheted three more stitches before Boots had the thread in her mouth again.

"That's it! I refuse to allow you to wreck Alice's birthday gift, especially as I am almost finished with it."

She put the crochet in the tote, and gathered up Boots, who went as limp as a furry rag. Annie started to place the cat on the porch floor, but paused when she heard a car pull into her driveway. She looked up and watched it approach as she absently stroked the cat's head. The driver was familiar, ruggedly handsome with graying hair and a winning smile. In spite of her age and experience, her heartbeat sped up like a schoolgirl's.

"Well, look who has come calling on us," she murmured to the cat. "The good mayor of our fair little town."

"Good morning, Annie—and Boots," Ian Butler called out as he stepped from the car and approached the porch steps.

"Good morning, Ian," Annie said, pleasantly surprised by his unexpected visit. If she had known Ian had planned to drop by, she would have at least styled her hair, powdered her nose and put on a little lipstick. She would have changed her clothes as well. Nothing she could do about that now, though. "Please join us."

She indicated the chair on the other side of the table and refused, absolutely *refused* to smooth her hair with her fingers, even though she was sure it was a fright being blown about by the sea breeze the way it was. There was not much she could do about her lack of lipstick, or her comfy old jeans and sweatshirt.

"You look lovely today," Ian said, smiling. "This cool, brisk wind brings out the color in your cheeks. But aren't you chilly out here?"

"Boots is keeping me warm," she said, returning his smile. He reached out and scratched the cat under her tiny chin. Boots stretched out her neck, closed her eyes half-way and purred like an outboard motor.

"Are you expecting a phone call?" he asked, nodding toward the phone on the small table next to her chair.

"Oh, you never know when someone will call. I'm so popular, you know." She laughed.

"Well, a terrific lady such as yourself will always be in demand."

She felt her face burn, hoping he knew she had only been joking about her popularity.

"I so enjoy being out here on the porch that I simply didn't want to get up and go into the house if someone should call," she explained. "Call me lazy."

He laughed. "Now that is something no one will ever call you, Annie Dawson. You inherited your grandmother's industry, along with her house and her cat."

She laughed again. "Thanks for saying so. Would you like some hot chocolate, Ian? Or some coffee?"

"Sure. Either one is fine; whatever is easier for you."

Annie threw off the afghan, got out of her chair, and without thinking twice about it, deposited the cat onto Ian's lap before she went inside. When she returned, Boots was sprawled across Ian's legs, tummy up, enjoying a rubdown.

"I thought my schnauzer was much indulged, but I believe this feline has Tartan beat," Ian told her as he accepted a large dark blue mug of hot chocolate. She had added a generous dollop of marshmallow crème on top.

"I refuse to accept the blame for spoiling that silly kitty," she told him with a laugh. "She was that way when I got her. That was either Gram's or Alice's fault. Here, let me take her. I'll put her in the house."

She picked up the cat, carried her to the door and settled her inside. Boots twitched her tail, looked insulted for a bit, and then regally strolled toward the kitchen in search of food.

"This is great," Ian said, after he took a drink. "Obviously not made from a mix the way I do."

"No. It's from scratch, but so easy to do. And it tastes better, I think."

"It certainly does," he agreed emphatically, and then discreetly used a crisp white handkerchief from his breast pocket to wipe a bit of marshmallow crème off his upper lip.

He glanced at the table runner when she picked it up again.

"And what have you there?"

She held it out. "A table runner. I made a couple of matching place mats, and I'm giving the set to Alice for her birthday. The Hook and Needle Club is having a surprise party for her next Tuesday." She gave him a conspiratorial look. "Don't you spill the beans!"

He raised one hand in a gesture of promise. "I would never dream of such a thing."

"Thank you, sir."

He smiled into her eyes.

"You are generous to spend so much time and thought— and hard work—on such a lovely gift. That is very sweet of you, Annie."

She felt her face grow warm again, so she turned from his gaze and focused on the crochet in her hands. As she resumed stitching, she changed the subject.

"You know, crocheting has long been one of the joys of my life," she said. "It always brings me closer to Gram." She glanced at him, smiled, and turned her attention back to working the corner of the runner. "She taught me how to do it when I was quite young. She was always so patient and encouraging. After all these years, anytime I get worried or stressed out by anything, I still find that I can lose myself with hook and yarn or thread. Crocheting helps me to relax."

Ian watched her busy fingers for a bit.

"I tend to eat cake when I feel stressed out," he said finally, with a rueful smile.

She slid a sideways glance at his trim physique.

"You must not feel under pressure very often, then."

He chuckled. "The secret is in the size of those pieces of cake. They must be very small. But, I must admit, I like your idea of being productive much better."

Once again, he watched her silently for a minute or so, and then asked, "So what's stressing you out, Annie?"

She glanced at him, startled. "What? Why do you say that? Has someone said something to you?"

"No one has said a word. But I can tell you have been—well—distracted. You didn't even wave at me yesterday when I saw you coming out of Malone's Hardware."

Her hands stilled their work. "Really? I didn't see you, Ian. Honest!"

"Even though you looked right at me, you didn't see me. That was quite clear."

His eyes twinkled, and she shook her head, smiling.

"I apologize for that. And you're right. I'm distracted. Very distracted."

"You have more repair problems here in the house? Maybe I can help." His voice trailed as she shook her head again.

"No," she said. "I mean, of course, I have repair problems. Don't I always? Thank God for Wally Carson. But Grey Gables's upkeep is not what has been on my mind lately."

Ian's expression turned from one that was slightly flirtatious to one of obvious concern. He leaned forward slightly.

"Nothing is wrong with your daughter, I hope?"

"Oh, no. LeeAnn is just fine, and so are Herb and the twins. In fact, I don't think I've talked to you since LeeAnn sent me that huge box of yarn."

"You didn't say a word about that. A box of yarn, eh? She couldn't have sent you anything that you would enjoy more, I think. Am I right?"

"You're right, Ian. But you should have seen that box! You should have been here that morning. Oh, my goodness, what an experience!" She told him the entire story, leaving out nothing from the time the delivery truck and its sullen driver arrived until she and Alice opened the box to find all those glorious contents. She concluded with, "But it was the search for something in which to keep all that yarn that has led me to this 'distraction' you mentioned."

"Ah. And that is … ?"

"Why don't I just show you? I'll be right back."

For the second time she set aside her crochet and went into the house. When she returned a minute later, Ian held her unfinished project in his hands, examining it closely as if he were trying to learn the pattern.

"I do *not* see how you do this," he said as she sat down. "It looks like a lot of hard work to me."

"That's exactly what Grandpa used to say to Gram and me. He would say, 'Why don't you two put that away for a while and rest?'" She smiled at the memory. "But nothing is hard work when you love what you do. Of course crocheting something as intricate as these place mats and table runner can be difficult. You have to take your time, and read the directions completely at least once before you plunge into it. And you surely can't be afraid to rip out stitches. I rip out stitches at a high rate every time I start a project." She laughed and shook her head. "Probably because I haven't mastered complete patience yet. I just get so excited to see it finished!"

Ian gave the piece one last perusal then handed it back to her.

"My Arianna would have loved that." The wistfulness in his voice stabbed Annie with its familiar lonely note. "She loved beautiful things."

She touched his hand with her fingertips, enough to convey a connection to that pain.

"It's tougher some days than others, isn't it?"

He hesitated, and then nodded. "Just about the time I think I am getting a handle on her being gone and me being alone ... well, something happens, and it is all fresh in my mind again. The unexpectedness of the aneurysm, the last time I saw her. All of it." He met her eyes. "You feel it too? About your husband, I mean?"

"Oh, yes! There are some days, especially lately ... ." She let her voice trail for a moment, and then said, "You know, I think the gloomy weather makes the lonesomeness worse, don't you?"

Ian's face crinkled around his eyes as he smiled.

"Now there's a word you don't hear every day in Stony Point. 'Lonesomeness.' And Annie, I surely agree that dreary days tend to bring out the most melancholy parts of me."

This is one reason Ian and I have such a good connection, Annie thought. *We have been through the same valley not so long ago.*

They sat in silence for a bit, looking out at the ocean

and the sky, the vast blueness that almost surrounded them together, but each one lost in their separate bittersweet memories.

"So what have you there?" Ian said after a while, fixing his gaze on the document in her hand.

She passed it to him.

"This was tucked in amongst a lot of other things Gram had packed away in that cedar chest Alice and I dragged out of the attic. Mike Malone promised to dig out some information for me, but his wife called last night to tell me he's laid up with a sinus infection for a few days. Poor guy. That can be so miserable."

Ian absently agreed as he scanned the first page. His eyes widened and he looked at the second page.

"Fairview!" he said.

"Yes. And I had never even heard of the place until I found that deed."

"Betsy never said anything about it to you?"

"Not a single word."

He read the first page again. "Who are Joseph and Alta Harper?"

"I was hoping you might know. I take it you don't."

Ian shook his head. "Never heard of them, and this was drawn up ... ." He squinted at the date. "Why, nearly thirty years ago! I was in college back then. Maybe that's why I don't remember them."

Annie sighed.

"Well, that is one of the problems. A big problem, in fact. No one remembers them. I'm beginning to think the Harpers never even lived here in Stony Point, even though

Fairview is listed as their address."

"Well, that's a thought. But maybe they came into ownership of the property through family." He flipped through the pages, "Did you see this name? David Ralston. The property was his from the 1920s until ownership transferred to Joseph and Alta in the 1950s. Before that, it was owned by Lincoln County."

She leaned near him to read the names he indicated. How had she missed that? Of course! Many deeds have previous owners listed!

"I feel utterly foolish," Annie said. "I saw Gram's name, and the Harpers' names, and that is where I stopped. I have just been … well, feeling so low this spring and then there was that wonderful gift from LeeAnn. Then the car broke down, and then there was that ghost hunt … . To tell you the truth, my thinking just has not been as keen as it should be lately."

Ian reached out and squeezed her fingers briefly.

"It's understandable, Annie. It really is. We all have the right to indulge in a little lapse from time to time. Why, last month I totally forgot—" He stopped short. "Wait a minute! Did you say 'ghost hunt?' What ghost hunt?"

Annie laughed and settled back, picked up the runner and worked a few stitches swiftly.

"Oh, Ian, you don't want to know about that, do you?"

"Are you serious?" he asked. "Of course I want to know."

She grimaced. "Well, just promise me that you will not think we are all a bunch of crazy ladies."

He gave her a peculiar look. "I'll do my best, Annie, but

the more you dangle these bits and pieces in front of me, the more intrigued I am."

She leveled a gaze at him. "Well, just remember: You asked for it!"

He grinned. "OK. I'll remember."

"Some of the Hook and Needle Club women have vowed and declared that Fairview is haunted."

He nodded. "That's been the prevailing notion around Stony Point for as long as I can remember."

"So we were finding out! The women at the Hook and Needle Club said that no one will want to buy a haunted house. Peggy Carson—that fount of ideas and wild notions—came up with this bright idea of us going out to Fairview so we can chase away all the ghosties and ghoulies. That way, according to her, I will be able sell the place, phantom-free."

Ian's eyebrows shot up.

"And you—level-headed, down-to-earth Annie Dawson—went along with that notion?"

She met his gaze and refused to be embarrassed, though it took great effort.

"Yep."

He stared at her a few moments longer, as though searching for remnants of her good sense, and then leaned back in his chair and laughed. Loud. And for a long time.

"Oh, Annie!"

"Umm hmm. You might say that."

"Well, don't just sit there. Tell me about this … caper."

"'Caper.' Now, that is the perfect word for it, Ian. I want you to know that, right in the middle of the Hook and Needle Club, Alice MacFarlane and Peggy Carson put their two little heads together and organized that whole 'caper.'" And she went on to tell him the details of their crazy jaunt to Fairview.

"You have never heard such squealing and screaming and faint-hearted pleadings. In all my life, if I had to make a bet on two women who would never run from dragons or monsters or anything else, Alice and Peggy would be those two women. Oh, Ian. They were a mess!"

They shared a hearty laugh, but eventually the laughter died.

"So," Ian said, after a bit, "I take it there are no ghouls or goblins out there."

"Nary a one," she assured him. "I can honestly tell any house shopper who might ask me about hauntings and suchlike, that as far as I know, Fairview does not have any ghosts. In fact, I'm about half tempted to have Mike publish it in the paper. But I have to admit, as crazy as that caper was, I am glad we did the investigation. We found out that something has set up housekeeping out there. Something of the four-legged nature that does not belong inside the house. Wally Carson is going to look into that for me."

"That's good. Wally will take care of it, I'm sure. I have to say, Annie, that I am glad none of you bold ladies got hurt out there."

"I think the house, as a structure, is pretty solid."

Ian nodded, but looked thoughtful and unconvinced.

"That's all well and good, but you never know. And don't forget, Annie, that Fairview is isolated enough to shelter … well, anyone looking for a place to hide."

His words raised prickles along her skin.

"You're right, of course. And please don't think I haven't thought about all that. But 'all's well that ends well,' I suppose. Thank you for being so concerned."

"Of course, I'm concerned. I like you, Annie. Just take care of yourself, all right?"

His words drew warmth to her heart, and she really needed that warmth.

"Thank you," she whispered.

Ian finished off his hot chocolate, and tapped the deed with his fingertip as he sat the cup aside. His expression was still sober and thoughtful.

"Something else concerns me, Annie," he said. The earnestness in his voice drew her attention and gave her pause.

"What's that?"

"Did you say you were going to sell Fairview?"

"Oh, yes. I don't want another old place to look after. Grey Gables is almost more than enough at times."

"I understand that. But, Annie." He waited until she looked up from her crochet to meet his eyes. He cleared his throat. "You might not own that property."

～13～

*I*an's words hit Annie like a sledgehammer. After all the rodent-infested, ghost-busting time she had spent at Fairview already—not to mention all of the repairs and renovations she was staring down in the not-too-distant future—she hadn't once considered the possibility that she might not have a clear title to Fairview. That seemed to be as clear as the deed Ian held in his hand.

"What do you mean? As far as I know, Gram left everything to me."

"That's all well and good." Ian tapped the deed with his fingertip. "But, Annie, please understand: Possession of a deed does not guarantee ownership."

The runner slipped unnoticed from her fingers and lay in a delicate heap on her lap. The steel hook pinged against the porch floor.

"Do you mean that maybe Gram never did own Fairview?"

"That's exactly what I mean."

"My goodness." She stared at him without seeing while this information penetrated her mind. "Then ... but ... why ... I mean ... ."

She gestured wordlessly at the deed.

"Why did Betsy have it?" he prompted. "Now *that*, my dear Annie, is a good mystery."

"Yes," she said faintly. "My goodness. As if there weren't enough mysteries surrounding the old place already."

Ian raised an eyebrow.

"Oh? There's more?"

"Why Gram has this deed, for one thing. And for another, why it was hidden away and never mentioned to me or anyone else? And why did she let Fairview get so run down? Just to name a few."

"I see. Well, Fairview was not always the run-down old wreck it seems to be now. It was rental property until, oh, about ten years ago. Not that the renters were great about keeping it up, but at least the grounds had been kept clean, and the house didn't have that awful look of abandonment about it."

"But I still don't understand … ." She sighed and looked out to the ocean. "I wish I could find the answers in those rolling, changing waves."

He followed her gaze.

"Wouldn't that be great, to find answers to all our problems and life's mysteries in the endless ebb and flow of the sea?"

"Yes," she sighed. "It would be such a comfort."

"Well, if it's any consolation, maybe I can help you a little. How about I get in touch with Will Green when I'm in Portland next week? He was a realtor here years ago. Maybe he remembers something."

She gave him a warm smile. "That would be great, Ian. Thank you."

"In the meantime, I suggest you go to the county recorder's office in Wiscasset and see if this deed was filed in your grandmother's name."

She took the deed from his hand, and stared down at it.

"How can such a little stack of papers cause such big problems?" she mused aloud.

"We'll get it sorted out, Annie, don't you worry. In the meantime, I came for a reason this morning."

Annie lifted her head, felt the sea breeze paw sweetly at her face. She took a deep breath, thinking she could smell the first greening of grass.

"What's that?" she asked him.

"I was hoping we could have dinner Saturday night."

She felt her eyes widen, although she did her best to stay cool and poised. Dinner? Like a date? She and Ian? They'd had casual lunches together on several occasions, but never an actual dinner date. He waited patiently for her answer, but she thought she saw beneath the surface a little uncertainty. Maybe he thought she would turn him down.

"That would be lovely," she finally said, gratified her voice did not betray her silly bout of nerves. After all, this was Ian Butler, a friend she had known now for a couple of years since moving to Stony Point. Nothing more. Just friends.

Her thoughts jumped immediately to most women's age-old question: *What will I wear?* On the heels of that query was: *I wish I had something new. Maybe I could run into town tomorrow and get something.*

"There's a new restaurant about halfway between here and Wiscasset that just opened a couple of days ago. Sweet Nell's. I thought it might be fun to check it out and would love for you to be my companion when I do."

Ian always had the nicest way of saying things. She turned her head for a moment so he would not see her cheeks pink up. Why was she acting like such a love struck puppy? He was her friend. Nothing more!

"Sure," she said, turning to him, giving him a smile. "I'd like that. Yes."

Oh my, listen to me, Annie thought. *And I wonder if he'll carry my books home from school. Grow up, Annie!*

"Great! I'll pick you up about seven?"

She cleared her throat delicately, and said quietly, with great decorum, "That would be just fine, Ian. Thank you."

He got to his feet, smiling down at her.

"See you then."

She inclined her head with what she hoped was graciousness.

"Yes. See you Saturday." And stopped herself from thanking him again.

Ian had just driven away when her phone rang.

"Good morning, Annie," a strange voice greeted when she picked it up.

She never liked getting phone calls when she could not identify the caller right away. She wished she had signed up for caller ID.

"Good morning," she said with courtesy and caution. "Who's calling?"

She heard laughter from the other end that turned into a cough, or maybe it was vice versa—she couldn't tell.

"It's Mike Malone," he croaked. "Excuse me a moment." He hacked and coughed again. "Sorry, Annie. This sinus infection has me sounding like my great-grandmother's favorite bullfrog. Can you hear me well enough?"

"I can hear you just fine, Mike, but I'm so sorry you

aren't feeling well. Can I do anything for you?"

Cough. "Nice of you to ask, but no. Just have to wait for the medicine to do its job." Cough, cough, wheeze. "Wish it would hurry up. Listen, I just wanted to tell you I haven't found anything regarding the Harpers, but I did find something about David Ralston, the original owner of Fairview."

A fit of coughing kept them both waiting until he could speak again.

"Mike, why don't we talk about this later, when you're feeling better?"

"No, no. I'm fine. Just a little croaky. What I found was just a mention in an old notebook someone wrote in 1931, and it says—" He hacked a bit more. "Scuse me. It says 'David Ralston recently bought a plot of heavily wooded land north of town and built a fine cottage. His business keeps him away, so it's unsure if he ever plans to live there. Perhaps he wants a holiday retreat and Fairview certainly will provide that for him.' That's all I've found, and I've gone through most of my records while I've been laid up. You know I can't stand to lie still."

This time the coughing went on until Annie was afraid for Mike's well-being.

"Mike!" she shouted above the sound of coughing. "Get off the telephone, and go lie down. I'll talk to you later."

He wheezed a reply, which she interpreted to be affirmative, and Annie broke the connection. She wondered if Mike's wife, Fiona, knew that he was up and shuffling through old records instead of recuperating while she was at work. She doubted it, but it was hard to keep a man like Mike Malone down. That restless drive to stay busy reminded her so much of Wayne that sudden, unexpected tears stung her eyes. She blinked them back and refused to give in to that familiar lonesomeness. *Lonesomeness.* Ian would probably smile at her use of the word again. Gathering her crochet tote, the phone and the two empty cups, she went inside to fix lunch.

Later, Annie sat in the window seat and munched her tuna sandwich while Boots watched every bite with unblinking green eyes.

It was hard for Annie to enjoy her meal when her mind kept rolling over the news that Gram might have had a deed to Fairview and yet not actually own the place. Could that possibly be the case? Would that be why Betsy never mentioned the property to anyone?

The need to know the answers bothered Annie so much that she decided there was no reason to sit around the house and wait while someone else did the investigating for her. She gave Boots the last quarter of her sandwich—bread, pickle, celery, and all—and went to change clothes and freshen up.

* * *

An hour later, Annie stepped through the doors of the lovely old brick courthouse in Wiscasset and found the county records office.

She presented the deed to the woman across the desk and said, "I need to know anything you can tell me about this property."

The woman quickly looked over the papers, and then

gave Annie a warm smile and said, "Sure. With our new computer system, we can find information about this in a flash for you."

Annie waited while the woman tapped the keys and scanned the screen. Finally, she gave a final click of the mouse and a nearby printer slid out a couple of pages. These she handed to Annie.

"There you are!" She tapped Betsy's name on the document. She leaned forward slightly, as if sharing a confidence. "Y'know, I just loved Betsy. And her cross-stitch work was just so ... mmm," she seemed to be searching for a word, "well, just so exquisite."

"You knew my grandmother?"

The woman's merry brown eyes widened. "You're her granddaughter? Oh, how interesting. And aren't you the lucky one to have been related! From your accent, I'd say you didn't grow up in Maine, though."

"No. I'm from Texas. But I spent summers up here with Gram."

"I see. Well, I didn't know Betsy very well, but I talked with her from time to time when she came into the courthouse. I ran into her at a craft shop in Portland once. She was always so nice and pleasant to visit with."

The words warmed Annie's heart. She hadn't spent as much time in the last several years with Gram as she should have, but it gratified her to know that others, even near-strangers, had regarded her grandmother with affection and respect.

"I'm wondering," she said, "if Gram ever talked to you about the place recorded on this deed? Fairview?"

The woman bunched her face as she pondered, and then she shook her head.

"I suppose it's possible that she did. But I just don't remember. We have so many property records that, truly, it is simply impossible to remember them all."

Annie hid her disappointment and said, "I understand."

She eagerly took the copies the other woman handed over, thanked her effusively, and then stepped aside so the woman could wait on the man who had entered the room shortly after Annie had. He now stood behind her, sighing loudly and shifting from foot to foot.

It only took Annie only a few moments to read the papers and learn what she had been longing to know.

That proves it! she thought. *Gram owned Fairview, free and clear, a gift from Joseph and Alta Harper of Stony Point, Maine.*

Except no one in Stony Point knew them. How could someone live in a place as small as that town and remain unknown?

Annie looked up from the papers, and as soon as the impatient man at the counter left, she once more approached the woman who'd helped her.

"I'm sorry to bother you again, but I have another question.

"What is it?"

"Do you happen to remember anyone named Joseph and Alta Harper?"

"Those are the other names on that-deed, aren't they? And I saw another name, David Ralston."

"Yes. Maybe you know something about him too?"

"Only that he bought the land from the county a long time ago, just as it says on the deed."

"But you know nothing about the Harpers?"

Again the woman scrunched her face in thought; again she shook her head.

"Sorry. I wish I could help."

"It was a long shot, and another dead end," Annie told her. "I seem to be running into a lot of those."

~ 14 ~

Diamond studs or delicate gold hoops? Maybe the dangling ones with pearls. Annie grimaced at her reflection. If she had had her ears pierced three times like LeeAnn did she could wear all three pair of earrings that now lay on her dresser and not have to choose.

Diamonds were always in style, of course, even small stones like the ones that caught the light and glittered up at her. Wayne had given her those earrings on Christmas the first year they were married. She smiled, remembering how proud he had been to give her diamonds. The hoops, simple and dressy, came from LeeAnn on Mother's Day just a few years ago. The dangling pearls were classic. She had bought them a couple of months ago from Alice at one of the Princessa jewelry parties in Stony Point. Annie touched each pair with a fingertip, trying to decide which ones to wear on that evening. Why was this so hard? She was purely disgusted with herself for letting a date with Ian Butler turn her into a ninny.

Date. What kind of word was that for someone of her age, anyway? Although, perhaps it applied more to Ian and her than to the younger set these days. She read somewhere that today's teenagers didn't "date." They "hooked up"—the term and its implications made her shudder—or they "hung out," a more benign activity, usually in groups.

But, in Annie's middle-aged world, dressing up and going out for the evening with a member of the opposite sex was considered a date.

She sighed and studied her hair again. Really, if she styled it in her customary bob, no one would even see her ears at all. Of course, if she combed it back, and tucked it sassily behind her ears, there were those lobes just hanging there for the entire world to see.

"Oh, for goodness sake!" she said.

She grabbed up a pair of black onyx cubes from her jewelry box on the dresser and put them on before she could second-guess her choice. She didn't even know where she had gotten those particular earrings, and more to the point, she didn't care.

At least she wouldn't have to worry about what clothes to wear. That morning she had gone to Dress to Impress and bought a lovely ice-blue sheath dress. With a crocheted wrap of shimmering cream-color silk and bone-color pumps, the complete outfit was simple and elegant. The black earrings added just the right touch of contrast.

As Annie gazed at herself in the full-length mirror, she was sure she would pass inspection. She was no raving beauty, but she was pretty sure she would not be too hard on anyone's eyes that evening.

As she gazed at her reflection, her thoughts turned to Wayne, how his face would light up when he saw her "all dolled up," as he liked to express it.

"Annie-girl," she could almost hear him say, "you look good enough to take to town."

She bit her lower lip. Was this date a good idea or not?

Was she ready for something like this with any man other than Wayne? And what about that niggling determination to keep things purely platonic between Ian and her? On the other hand, did she want to go through the rest of her life as "just friends?"

The front doorbell rang startling her a little. Was she ready? Nervous, yes. Cold hands, thumping heart, completely uncertain she was doing the right thing, Annie once more met her own eyes in the reflection and looked far into their depths.

"You can't allow yourself to stagnate, Annie Dawson. Or to dry up on the vine. This date does not mean you and Ian are going to elope tonight. It's just dinner. Go out and have a good time."

The reasonable sound of her own voice helped Annie regain control. She fluffed her hair, leaned forward to check her lipstick, made a final pirouette in front of the mirror to make sure her stockings sported no runs or snags.

"You'll do," she said. "Now get out there and have a good time. And for goodness sake, stop talking to yourself!"

Ian's eyes widened when she opened the door.

"Why, Annie!"

He was dressed far more casually than she was, in khaki slacks and white buttoned- down oxford shirt, open collar, no tie.

"You're a vision!" he said.

She took a step back and invited him inside. She felt foolish and gawky—and terribly overdressed.

"I'll just … run upstairs and put on something less dressy. Wait right here. No, I mean, please have a seat in the living room and I'll—"

"Annie!" he laughed, reaching for her arm. "Hold on. You look lovely. Please don't change."

"Oh, but—"

"But nothing! If you change so much as an earring, we'll go to Weenie World."

Her mouth dropped open.

"You would not dare take me there. No one but high school kids goes to Weenie World."

He shrugged. "I'm a kid at heart. So … you gonna change out of that lovely blue dress? By the way, I hear the chili dogs will give you heartburn."

She shook her head and laughed at him.

"Not if it means you're taking me for chili dogs and greasy tater tots. No way."

"Great. Then let's go." He opened the front door. "I'm glad to see you have that beautiful shawl. It's nippy outside."

"At least the snow from the other day melted quickly," she said as they walked outside.

"Yes. I'm looking forward to spring."

"It's one of my four favorite seasons," she said.

"Mine too. See? I've always known we have a kinship of minds."

They chatted about the weather all the way to his car, and almost to the Stony Point city limits. Annie realized weather was a weak topic, useful to fill time when no one has anything else to say. She cast about in her mind for a new subject.

"Read any good books lately?" she blurted, interrupting his observations about the month of August.

Ian shot her a sideways look and then focused on the road ahead.

"I don't have a lot of time for reading, but I've been working my way through John Grisham's novels."

"I never had much time for reading when I lived in Texas. Work took up most of my day. But I've found time to read since moving to Stony Point."

"When you aren't crocheting, you mean," he prompted with a smile.

"Yes. When I'm not crocheting."

"Did you make that shawl?"

She looked down at the silken wrap, fingered it lovingly.

"Yes. Gram bought me the yarn and helped me get started on it one summer." She laughed lightly. "I guess you could say it's an antique, it's been so long ago since I made it."

Ian reached out, touched a strand of fringe. It slid through his fingers.

"It's as beautiful as the lady who crafted it."

The words, spoken so softly, sent a shiver across her skin. She shifted in her seat, drew the shawl more snugly around her.

"Cold?" Ian said. "I'll turn up the heater."

Warm air rose from the car's heating vents and comforted her. Annie was not sure if she liked Ian's less-than-subtle flirting. In fact, she thought he was going beyond mere flirting and into a territory she preferred to avoid. Once again she changed the subject.

"So you've never been to this place we're going. What did you say it was called?"

"Sweet Nell's. I haven't been there yet, but I've heard

the food is good and the entertainment is pretty good."

"Entertainment? You mean like a dinner theater? Oh, what fun! I've always loved live theater."

Ian was very quiet and kept his attention on his driving.

"Ian, is it a dinner theater?"

"Umm," he stalled. "Not exactly."

"What do you mean 'not exactly'?" She frowned, thought about it, and didn't like what came into her mind. "Now, wait a minute. Ian! You aren't taking me to one of those … those awful places where—"

"No! Annie, I'm surprised at you even thinking such a thing. I think I'm a little hurt, actually."

She bit her lip and studied his profile. He didn't look hurt. His brows were pulled down, but he didn't appear angry either. In fact, he looked as if he had some sort of hilarious secret.

"Ian? Why do I get the notion you've just swallowed a canary?"

He laughed.

"No canaries. Look, there's Sweet Nell's just ahead."

She looked, leaned forward and looked harder.

"That's that old abandoned tire shop, isn't it?"

"It used to be, yes."

"And now it's a restaurant?

He snickered again as he slowed the car and flipped on the right-hand turn signal.

"Well, they've renovated it, of course."

She leaned back and eyed the structure as they pulled into the brightly lit parking lot. The metal building had been painted a clean fresh color—in the dark, she couldn't tell what color it was—maybe pale blue, maybe gray, perhaps off-white. The old rusted metal door had been replaced with large, double glass doors, and the light from inside spilled cheerfully across the entrance.

"There are a lot of cars," she observed as Ian parked. "I suppose you had to make reservations?"

"I don't think we'll need them. It's a big place."

He got out and went around the car to open her door. He offered his hand as she stepped out. It was a good thing he did so because the heels of her pumps did not take kindly to the rock parking lot. Clinging to his strong hand, Annie stepped carefully until they reached the sidewalk.

"You can hear the music all the way out here," she said, and immediately regretted the dismay in her voice.

Ian stopped, tilted his head slightly as he looked at her.

"We can go somewhere else, Annie. I chose Sweet Nell's because I thought you needed something fun to do. You've seemed so … oh, I don't know, a little blue lately, and I've heard this place is fun. But I don't want you to be uncomfortable. We can drive on to Portland, or back toward Wiscasset, if you'd like."

His expression was so kind and so caring that she reached out and brushed his cheek quickly, lightly with the fingertips of one hand.

"Thank you, Ian. And you're right. After these last few weeks of allowing myself to give into loneliness and frustration and confusion, I do need some fun. My friends in Stony Point are fun. Crocheting is fun. Even investigating Fairview's history and Gram's part in it has been fun, in its own way. But I need something new and different to do." She smiled into his eyes. "I apologize for being such a 'diva'."

"Diva! You mostly certainly are not. Divas are spoiled and unreasonable."

She smiled in relief.

"Thanks for saying so, Ian. I don't like to be around whiners." She glanced through the glass doors into the crowded restaurant. "I'd like to see what Sweet Nell's has to offer."

"You're sure?"

"One hundred percent!"

"Great!" He reached out and opened the door for her.

She stepped into a warm building full of the smells of perfume and good food to be met by the worst music Annie had ever heard in her life. It was not only loud, but the singer was terribly off-key and fumbling for lyrics. She looked questioningly at Ian. He wriggled his eyebrows comically.

"Good evening!" someone greeted.

She turned to see a cheerful, plump young man approach. His long-sleeved blue T-shirt sported the graphic of a mic-holding female singer on the front with "Sweet Nell's" emblazoned above the image in glittering letters.

Was Sweet Nell the singer who screeched so pathetically from the stage? Annie sincerely hoped not.

Since the young greeter wore blue jeans and sneakers, Annie felt more over-dressed than ever. She wished Ian had let her change before they left Grey Gables.

"Just two of you this evening?" the young man asked.

"Yes. Just the two of us." Ian smiled down at Annie.

"This way, please."

Annie glanced around as they followed him through a

maze of full tables. The restaurant, decorated in retro chic, boasted a variety of old chrome dinette tables with red-checked tablecloths. On the walls, neon signs advertised everything from soft drinks to baking powder. As far as the appearance of the place, Annie felt right at home. In Texas, she had often eaten down-home comfort food in little mom-and-pop diners like this one. Without the stage, of course.

The young man settled them slightly apart from the other diners.

"Your server will be along in just a moment. The song choices are listed in the display on your table. Have a great evening."

"Song choices?" She looked at the little carousel of titles and then turned to stare at Ian. He looked back, eyes twinkling, and a smile trying to free itself.

"Annie?" he said, hopefully.

"Karaoke! Ian, for goodness sake!" She laughed.

"Can you sing?"

"Of course I can sing. At home. At church. In my garden. But never, ever in front of a room full of strangers."

"Um-hmm." He merely gaze at her and waited as if he expected her to change her mind.

"Ian, I am *not* going to get up in front of people and make a fool of myself. No!"

His gaze never wavered from hers, but the smile came, filling his face with merriment.

"OK, then. But will it bother you if I do?"

She lifted her eyebrows. "Really? You want to?"

"Sure. Why not? If you look around you'll see that these people in here are our friends and neighbors. I'll enjoy it, and they'll get a kick out of hearing Stony Point's mayor get down and funky."

She nearly choked on her water.

"'Down and funky?' Who are you, anyway? Rick James?"

He laughed so hard that the couple at the next table looked at them.

A bit later, after they'd studied the menu, the waiter—who'd said his name was Steve—took their order without writing down a word of it. He slipped off almost as quickly as he had arrived.

Annie glanced at the other diners. Nearly everyone wore jeans, khakis, or other comfort wear, and she was pretty sure her pumps were the only pair in the entire building.

She told herself feeling awkward or conspicuous was silly, and certainly pointless. After all, the looks cast her way had all been friendly, and for the most part, admiring. At one point, a youngish red-haired woman approached their table.

"Excuse me for interrupting," she said with an apologetic smile, "but I've been admiring your shawl since you came in. I'd love to have one like that. Where did you buy it, if you don't mind me asking?"

"I don't mind you asking, but I didn't buy it. I made it."

The woman's eyes rounded.

"No! Really? Are you sure?"

Annie laughed. "I'm positive. I remember crocheting every stitch."

The redhead looked at it and sighed. Then she reached into her purse and pulled out a business card. She handed it to Annie.

"If you ever make more, I want to buy one. Please. Call me. Or e-mail. I'd just love to have one so much. Maybe someday you'll want to get rid of this one." She touched it wistfully.

Annie took the card, smiled, and said, "I'll surely give you a call if I make any more."

"See?" Ian said, after the woman went back to her own table. "If you hadn't worn that gorgeous shawl, that lady would not have anything to sigh over tonight."

She tucked the card into her wallet with the intention of passing it on to Kate. Annie followed patterns, and she did it well, but Kate was a true crochet craftsman.

"I suppose you're right. A lot of people seem to have noticed it."

She was glad she had made something so lovely that others enjoyed looking at it. But all the same, when their salads arrived, she was relieved to have her mind on food instead of her appearance.

"My goodness," she said as she watched Ian heap Thousand Island dressing onto his fresh greens. "I haven't had Thousand Island dressing since I was a teenager."

"Why's that?" he asked, ripping open a hot roll from the bread basket between them.

"Calories, of course." She grinned.

"Did you like it?"

"The dressing? Oh, yes. Thick and creamy, kind of sweet with just a hint of tartness. It used to make all that lettuce go down a little easier."

She reached for the vinaigrette. Ian caught her hand.

"You don't need to always watch calories. Tonight, Annie,

have the Thousand Island. And hot rolls. With butter."

Tempted by the suggestion, she bit her lower lip and thought about it. She had always tried to be careful with her diet, though she indulged herself from time to time. Ian was right. Tonight was a night to relax and have fun. That was the whole purpose of this date, wasn't it? To have fun?

"OK. Pass it over! And the butter too."

She dolloped the dressing with a generous hand, spread the soft roll with pure butter, and when her meal came, she ate every morsel of baked potato, T-bone steak, and cheesy broccoli casserole. The change of fare from seafood to beef suited her that night. She was a Texas girl, after all.

"Dessert?" Ian asked her just as Steve the Waiter approached again.

"I'm stuffed," she admitted, "but..." She looked at Steve. "Do you have chocolate cake?"

"House specialty. Nell's Death by Chocolate Cake."

"Ooo! Sounds marvelous. I'll have some of that."

"Make it two pieces," Ian told him. To Annie, he said, "I'm proud of you!"

"I may have to waddle out of here, but I have enjoyed every single one of those calories."

"I'll be waddling with you."

They shared a laugh, and then she said, "I have a question, Ian."

He raised an eyebrow. "Yes?"

"Who is Sweet Nell?"

"I'm not positive, but I think Nell was the name of the owner's tabby cat when he was a boy."

"I see. Well, that's sweet. A little odd, but sweet."

While they'd been enjoying dinner, the music had continued almost nonstop. A few good singers had performed, but mostly nerves or lack of talent had kept the performances less than stellar. At long last a lull in music from the small stage gave the entire restaurant a new ambiance. Best of all, no one had to speak loudly to be heard.

Ian finished his cake and sipped half a cup of coffee; then he got to his feet.

"Annie, I'm about to go on. Are you sure?"

She looked up at him, eyes wide. "About not singing, you mean? I'm positive. And especially after that big meal … no, I'll stay put, thanks. But, please. You just go right ahead."

She watched him walk confidently toward the stage, admired his trim physique, and how the light shone on his silvery hair. Ian was an attractive man, and that was putting it mildly. Resting her chin on her hands, she sighed and smiled dreamily.

He stepped up onto the stage, tinkered a bit with the electronics, picked up the microphone and waited for the music to start.

The diners stopped speaking as soon as he barreled into a song Annie had never heard before. It was lively, engaging … and on key. She loved it.

"Woo-hoo!" shouted a table full of young people, their expressions surprised, their faces beaming. Annie assumed the song must be a hot one. No wonder she hadn't heard it. She listened to classic rock or jazz.

Ian stayed on the stage when the song ended. When the cheering died, his beautiful baritone voice filled the room with an oldie from the fifties, *Young at Heart*. Finally, looking at Annie, he sweetly sang *You've Got a Friend*.

Tears stung her eyes. Before Ian had finished the song, those tears had spilled over and slid down her cheeks, tracking through her makeup. She didn't care. She had needed to hear it: the tender comfort from a message of loyalty and friendship, in the genuine, simple way he delivered it to her. She no longer cared that others looked at her in curiosity. Prolonged and loud applause followed him, along with every eye in the place as he returned to their table. The diverted attention allowed Annie the time to gather herself and wipe away the tears—and what was left of her mascara.

"Great!" said a man a few tables away. Ian paused to shake his hand.

A woman called, "You can really sing, Mr. Mayor!"

"You rock, Mayor Butler!" This came from the teenagers across the room.

A fine sheet of sweat covered his face as he sat down, and he mopped it away with his napkin.

"A little warm under those lights," he muttered.

"My goodness, Ian!" Annie said, gaping at him. "I had no idea you could sing like that. No wonder you wanted to come tonight. You've missed your calling."

He laughed. "What? You don't think I'm a good mayor?"

"You're a wonderful mayor, but you're a great singer too. Wow!" She shook her head. "I loved the song choices."

"Well, I chose them because of their messages, not to show off my ability."

"They touched me. I needed to hear all of them. Thank you."

He pressed her hand briefly. "You are more than welcome, Annie. And maybe next time, you'll sing …?"

"That's not going to happen, Ian. So, tell me, I'd never heard that first song choice before."

"That was *Home*, by Edward Sharpe and the Magnetic Zeros. It was the official summer song of a Boston area 'young person' radio station last year. I heard it, liked it and wanted to sing it."

"No wonder those kids went crazy over it."

"Yeah. Kids."

Several constituents from Stony Point collected around the table to commend him and shake his hand.

"Annie!" a white-haired woman she barely knew said. "You've certainly made a fine catch for yourself. A mayor and singing star, all wrapped up into one nifty package. Not to mention he's the most handsome single fellow in Stony Point, Maine!"

Annie flushed from the roots of her hair to the tips of her toes. Did people really think she had "caught" Ian? She was almost too embarrassed to look at him, but he laughed lightly.

"Now, Clara," he said, "I'm thinking you've cast a pretty straight line for Calvin, haven't you?"

It was Clara's turn to blush.

"Why, Ian Butler! Calvin is just a friend, and you know it." She cleared her throat and patted her hair. "I was just teasing Annie, of course. She looks so lovely tonight. Well, see you later." She was gone in a flash.

"I hope she didn't embarrass you too much, Annie," he said. "She's always going on about things like that."

"I know." Annie nodded. But she was embarrassed all the same, and she hoped no one else in town thought she had been chasing after Ian. Or any other man for that matter.

The drive home was quiet. The awkwardness Clara had introduced seemed to linger, right up to the time Ian walked Annie to her front door.

She held out her right hand, and said, "Thank you, Ian, for a lovely evening."

He took her head and squeezed it gently. One could hardly call it a handshake.

Afraid he might try to kiss her, she took a step back, drew out her key and fumbled for the lock.

"I had a good time, Annie," he said. "Maybe we can do this again?"

She heard the optimism in his voice and saw the warm light in his eyes. She shoved down her own swell of hope and refused to acknowledge she felt it. She turned the key and opened the door.

"Thanks again, Ian. Have a good night."

Before he could say another word, she slipped inside like the coward she was and fled upstairs.

That evening was the first one in quite some time that she hadn't given Fairview a moment's thought, and the old house was not what was on her mind the rest of the night.

The sound of Ian's singing lingered in her head as she drifted into sleep.

— 15 —

"Hello, ladies," Annie said as she entered A Stitch in Time Tuesday morning.

"Well, I see you survived," Stella greeted cryptically, already clicking away on a multicolored slipper. "And look!" She stopped knitting, reached into her tote and pulled out a completed slipper, which she held up proudly. "Like falling off a bicycle!"

"That's 'like riding a bicycle,' Stella," Alice said, laughing.

The older woman waved off the comment, chuckling. "You know what I mean."

"It's adorable," Annie said. "Cable-stitched, right? I love it. We all knew you could make slippers."

Annie settled down and pulled out the deep red yarn she chose for the pair she was going to make. She planned to trim them with a scalloped border of pure white.

"Did you finish the table runner?" Alice asked.

"I did."

"Did you bring it?"

"No. Just the yarn and slipper pattern."

Alice made a pouty face.

"Then I'll just have to pop over to your house to see it, won't I? Why on earth would you tease us with that beautiful set all this time and not bring in the finished project?"

The others shared secretive smiles. Orange cloud punch

and orange coconut butter cake sat in the refrigerator of the store's back room, waiting to be served at Alice's surprise party when the meeting ended. Bright gift bags and cheerfully wrapped presents lay on the table, covered by a dust sheet, in case Alice needed to make a visit to the "facilities." Best of all, Alice remained clueless about the whole event.

"So, you three ladies," Mary Beth said, looking from Annie to Alice to Peggy, "we're all curious as barn cats about your adventure out to Fairview. We know you survived—for which we're very thankful, by the way—but now that all four of you hardy explorers are here, we want to hear all about your foray into the world of the paranormal." She smiled at Kate, who was dusting off a display carousel of novelty buttons. "Kate told me she went along, and you had a lot of fun, but she flatly refused to give me any details."

"Kate went to Fairview?" Stella and Gwendolyn chimed together. They fastened twin astonished gazes on the younger woman.

"Yes," Kate said, smiling at the entire group. "It was … an experience."

The quartet of "adventurers" shared glances and expressions. None of them wanted to let the others know exactly how a certain duo reacted that night, and yet the tale would be incomplete without it.

"We had a blast!" Alice said.

"But if it hadn't been for Kate, we'd have left *much* too soon," Peggy blurted.

Stella's gaze sharpened. "What do you mean?"

Before anyone else could say a word, Peggy launched into an accurate account of the evening. She hid nothing and concluded with, "And Wally is out at Fairview right now, looking for whatever has nested in the walls or attic or wherever it has nested."

"My goodness!" Gwen said. "I'm torn between relief of missing all that 'merriment,' and jealousy that you had such an adventure while I languished at home, trying to recover from a root canal."

Alice pinned a look on Kate.

"I want to know about your previous ghost experience."

"What?" Stella and Gwen said.

Mary Beth sniffed. "Kate is too level-headed for that kind of nonsense."

"That's not what she told us the other night," Peggy said. "Go on, Kate. Tell us. You said you would."

Kate looked uncomfortable, and Annie saw no reason to force her into talking about something she wanted to keep to herself.

"Why don't we leave her alone, ladies? This is obviously something she would rather not discuss."

"But she promised!" Alice said.

"Ummm … I don't remember any promise."

Peggy folded her arms, and Alice pooched out her lower lip in a pout. Both she and Alice stared at Kate.

"Would you look at the two of you?" Annie said. "Both of you scared spitless by some whistling wind, and yet here you are, begging to hear about more 'ghostly encounters.'"

They shifted their mutinous glares from Kate to Annie.

Kate said, "Thanks for sticking up for me, Annie. I'll tell the story sometime, when I'm in the mood."

"Oh, for heaven's sake! I've heard enough." Stella picked

up her needles once more. "Your excursion to Fairview was an entertaining story, and as Mary Beth said, we're glad none of you were hurt. But I've heard enough about wind through cracks disguised as spooks and ghouls. What I want to know is what Annie found out about the place since last week."

"Me too," said Mary Beth.

"Yes, tell us," Peggy said, forgetting her grudge. "Details. We're dying for details."

Annie sighed audibly.

"I know you want to know more. I want to know more, but it seems I just keep running into dead ends. I went into Wiscasset the other day, and all I found out was that Gram owned the place—"

"Didn't you already know that?" Kate asked.

"Well, I thought so. But then, Ian told me that possession of a deed did not necessarily prove ownership. You know, I almost hoped she *didn't* own it."

"I certainly understand that." Stella's needles clicked and flashed in the light. She never looked up. "Who wants such an old eyesore, anyway?"

"But Gram did own it. There it was, in black and white. The property was given to her by Joseph and Alta Harper, but the only address for them was Fairview. And of course, there was the original owner of the place, David Ralston."

Stella looked up with a frown. "You have never mentioned David Ralston before."

Annie gave them a shame-faced smile.

"I feel embarrassed to admit this, but actually, once I saw the Harpers' names and then read that Gram got the place from them, I just stopped examining that deed."

Stella pinned a steely gaze on her.

"Annie Dawson! And you're a businesswoman."

"You're right," she said. "I have no excuse. But now I know, and it still doesn't help."

"Who owned it before this Ralston fellow?" Gwen asked.

"The county, apparently. David Ralston bought the land from the county. Do any of you know anything about him?"

"Never heard of him," Stella said crisply.

"No," said Mary Beth and Gwen, and the others just shook their heads.

Annie sighed again, crocheted furiously for a bit, and then added, emphatically, "Well, I'm not giving up."

"And you shouldn't give up!" Stella said this rather loudly, Annie thought.

"In fact, I think we, as a group, should help you."

"Why, Stella! That would be great."

"I've been thinking about it for a few days," the older woman said. "We all know how Betsy kept every tidbit and scrap that came across her path ... ."

She looked around, waiting for their agreement. Everyone nodded.

"Annie," she asked, "are there dressers and chests and boxes at Fairview where information might be stored?"

"Sure. The house is fully furnished. But according to Ian there were renters there until about ten years ago."

Stella drew her spine straighter than ever and looked over the tops of her glasses at Annie.

"Really?" As if she did not believe her.

"That's what Ian told me."

"And Mr. Mayor would not lie," Peggy declared.

"Of course not! I didn't say that he would. But I just find it hard to believe that anyone lived in that old place … ."

"Ian said he was going to talk to someone in Portland who used to sell real estate here. Maybe he'll know something."

"Will Green?" Mary Beth asked.

"I believe that was the name, yes."

"Well, if anyone would know, it'd be him. He was about the nosiest person I've ever met."

The women exchanged surreptitious glances, and then bent their heads busily over their projects. No one would say what they were all thinking: *It takes one to know one!*

"After the party, I say let's all go out there and see what we can find," Stella said.

Annie's head shot up, along with everyone else's in the entire Hook and Needle Club. Stella's eyes widened as she caught her gaffe too late.

"Party?" Alice said. "What party?"

No one said anything, but they did a lot of shifting and rustling of yarn, fabric and thread without looking at her. Kate wafted toward the back room.

"Hey!" Alice said. "What party?"

"Uh … umm." Annie tried to think fast.

"Are you guys throwing me a surprise birthday party?" Alice said, half-grinning, half-wary.

No one said anything because apparently no one wanted to be the one to out-and-out spoil the party Mary Beth had been planning for the last two weeks.

"Okay, yes!" Mary Beth said finally. "After the meeting today."

Alice's expression went from laughing to soft and mushy as if they were a litter of roly-poly puppies.

"You guys! Really? That's so sweet." She shot a look at Stella. "And Stella, aren't you the sly one?"

Stella sniffed and squirmed.

"Well, apparently not too sly, letting it slip that way." Her shoulders drooped for a moment, and she looked at the others. "I am so sorry!"

"I'm not!" Alice declared. "In fact, I say let's close this meeting early and get on with the celebration. It's not every day someone my age turns my age again."

They all laughed with her, and after a brief discussion of slipper needs, Mary Beth dismissed them, went to the front door, locked it, turned the open sign around and closed the shop.

"I don't do this for just anyone," she said, giving Alice a quick hug. "And we can't keep the shop closed all day. But for now, we're going to have a party, with no interruptions. Ladies, follow me to the back room."

* * *

After the cake was no more than half a cake with holes where candles used to be, the presents unwrapped with *oohs* and *ahhs*, and the punch bowl empty of the orange cloud punch, the ladies straightened the stockroom and drifted out the front door, back to their regular routines. No one mentioned anything more about going to Fairview.

Annie had just reached the Malibu when a familiar sleek car pulled into the parking space next to hers.

Ian smiled at her through the windshield and then got out.

"Good afternoon, Annie!"

Rather than being pleased to see him, Annie felt embarrassed and foolish. Her abrupt departure Saturday had been rude and completely uncalled for. She had no idea how to make up for such idiotic behavior.

"Hi, Ian," she said in a small voice.

He stuffed both hands into his pockets and leaned his lower half against the front of his car. He eyed the tote in her hand.

"Been to the Hook and Needle Club meeting, eh?"

She nodded. "We're making slippers."

He hitched up an eyebrow.

"I mean, we're making slippers for the residents of Seaside Hills Assisted Living. That's our current project. I mean, our current project involves them. That is, our project is to make slippers. Stella is knitting some. And of course, Kate is crocheting. And you know I'll be crocheting." She stopped speaking abruptly when she realized she was prattling like a teenager.

Ian gave her a definite look of concern. "Annie, are you all right?"

"I'm fine. Just fine. It's such a lovely day, isn't it? I love spring, when everything is so fresh." She was babbling again. She gazed down the street helplessly for a moment, and then turned her attention fully to Ian. "I want to apologize for the other night. I ... well, I was rude."

He frowned and looked confused.

"What do you mean? I thought we had fun the other

night. You didn't enjoy yourself?"

"My goodness, yes! Going to Sweet Nell's was a great experience, something new. But I slammed the door in your face. More or less."

He laughed. "What? Were you afraid I was going to try to kiss you?"

She felt blood heat her face, but she kept her head up and faced down her discomfiture.

"Yes," she said. "And I'm not ready for that."

They stared at each other, and Annie realized she had just killed any romance that might have been tender on the vine with Ian. She ignored the stab that shot straight through her heart.

"Well, Annie. I appreciate your honesty. I'm not sure I'm ready for anything like that myself."

Had she misread his signals from that night? Obviously she had. A little disappointed but rather relieved, she smiled.

"Oh! Well, then. It's all good, isn't it?"

"Yes. It's all good. And I have something for you." He turned, taking a yellow legal pad out of his car, and glanced down at it. "I talked to Will Green yesterday."

"Oh, good! I hope you have some information for me."

"I do. It isn't much, but it will help you, maybe." He took his glasses out of his breast pocket and slipped them on. "I took notes so I wouldn't forget." He looked at her over the tops of the glasses. "This is too important to you for me to forget details."

She laughed. "Ian, you have the memory of an elephant. How could you run Stony Point, if you forgot things?"

He shrugged, grinned.

"Age, my dear girl, creeps up on us all. Besides, I have staff whom I trust to remember things for me."

He turned to the paper, shook it a little as though to shake out any wrinkles, and read silently for a moment. Annie waited, trying to keep a lid on her curiosity and impatience.

"The house—Fairview—was rented out to Millie Pratt in 1989 until her death ten years later. Will worked with Betsy to contract housekeeping and groundskeepers for the place because Miss Pratt was elderly and disabled. She apparently was alone in the world, quite poor, and Betsy provided furnishings, utilities, and charged a mere pittance for rent. Probably just enough to salvage Miss Pratt's pride."

Excitement ran so strongly through Annie that she dropped her tote. She scooped it up in a frenzy, laughing.

"That was Gram's way, you know. She liked to take care of folks. So Will Green has all the information I need?"

Her high spirits plummeted when she saw Ian's expression.

"I'm sorry. Will was under a strict agreement that prior ownership of Fairview should remain anonymous, and all he knew was that Betsy owned it. He didn't know any details of how or why she had the property, or even who had owned it before her."

"Oh. Oh, dear."

"I'm sorry you're disappointed, Annie. I wish I had better news. Or at least more news. I know how much you want to find out about the place."

"Thanks, Ian," she sighed. "And please don't apologize. I appreciate that you uncovered as much as you did." She sighed again, and then asked, "I'd still like to know why the place got run down. That just was not like Gram."

"From what I deduced, it seems she kept it up for a while, trusting someone else with the upkeep, but just decided it was too much."

"Then why didn't she sell it?"

"Now that," he said, "I can't tell you."

"It would be the logical thing to do."

"It would. I'm sure she had her reasons, though. Betsy Holden was no fool."

"You're right," she replied with a bright smile. "She was the smartest, kindest woman I knew. If I'd been around more those last few years of her life … ."

"Now, Annie, don't start to think that way. You did what was best for your family. Betsy took good care of herself, and she had friends up here who looked out for her. If any of us had known about Fairview, we would have helped her sort things out. For whatever reason, she chose to tell no one. Looking into the past now and dredging up guilt doesn't change a thing, and you know it does absolutely no good for anyone."

She met his eyes, and allowed their warmth to lightly squeeze her heart.

"Thanks, Ian. You are a good friend."

"I try." He looked over his shoulder toward A Stitch in Time and changed the subject. "So how'd the party go?"

She laughed. "It was great! Alice was surprised, but the surprise came when Stella spilled the beans right in the middle of our meeting."

"Good ol' Stella," he laughed. "And did she like that crocheted lacy bit you made for her?"

"The table runner and place mats. Yes, she *loved* them.

In fact, she broke down and cried because each one of us had given her something unique and handmade that she had really wanted."

"And cake?"

"The best orange-coconut cake ever, even if Alice didn't bake it with her own capable hands."

"That's saying something. Her desserts are always phenomenal."

He glanced at his watch and pushed away from the car.

"Well, Annie, I have a meeting in less than ten minutes at City Hall."

"Then you'd better run along. Thanks so much for talking with Will Green for me."

"It was my pleasure. I'll see you again." He smiled at her, went around his car and got in. Annie stood where she was, watching him back out and drive away.

"I'm not ready for that kind of thinking," she muttered as unwanted and rather romantic notions popped into her mind. It was better for her to concentrate on Grey Gables, her crochet work, the Hook and Needle Club, and Fairview. Ian Butler must remain exactly what he was: a good friend.

～ 16 ～

At the next meeting, Annie filled in the Hook and Needle Club members on information Ian had gleaned for her. "I still say we go out there and see what we can find." Stella said, somewhat loudly. "You all know as well as I do that Betsy filled any drawers, boxes or chests out there with more stuff."

Although the mere thought of prowling through more miscellanea made Annie's head ache, she tended to agree with the older woman.

"Well, I'm game if you are," she said, finishing off the blue-striped slipper. It completed the third pair she had made. It was such fun and so satisfying to share LeeAnn's gift this way.

"I think we should all go," Gwen said. "As long as it's safe. I have no desire to fall through the floor."

"No one is going to fall through any floor," Peggy said stoutly. "My Wally went over the house with a fine-tooth comb last week."

Wally had told Annie all the details of his findings, but right then she gave Peggy the floor to share the information with the other ladies. While Peggy talked, Annie started the foundation chain for another pair of slippers.

"The roof needs to be replaced, but it's not going to fall in," Peggy said. "The floor is solid; good hardwood there. The windows need to be caulked and sealed, the broken ones replaced. A mason should tuck-point the broken mortar in the fireplace. And those scurrying footsteps, glass and rattling noises? At some point, pack rats have been in the attic and in the walls. They've brought in every conceivable thing you can think of—even broken pieces of glass. What Wally found was a multigenerational nest of raccoons and mice."

Alice let out a little shriek of disgust and dismay. Peggy gave her a look.

"The noise of us being there," Peggy continued, dragging her gaze from Alice, "frightened them and they scampered. Wally is using a live trap so he can 'catch and release' out in the woods, far from the house."

"And he's going to repair all those holes and entry points so they can't return," Annie added.

"Yes. And then do all the other things that need to be done."

"And then what?" Gwen asked. "Are you going to rent it out, Annie? It would be a great rental for summer people."

Annie wrinkled her nose slightly. "I think the title of landlady wouldn't sit well on my shoulders. I'd rather sell it."

"I still want to go out there!" Stella insisted. "You have established that it's unlikely I'll break a hip by falling through a rotten floor, so I'm ready for an adventure … watered down, certainly, but an adventure just the same."

Annie looked around at the others. "Far be it from me to deny Stella a watered-down adventure. How about the rest of you? Do you want to prowl around Fairview?"

The rest of them enthusiastically agreed, fidgeting and

chattering with anticipation.

When they quieted, Annie said, "Mary Beth, after you close the shop, why don't we all meet here and ride out there?"

"It will be getting dark by then," Gwen piped up. "Let's go Sunday afternoon instead. If it isn't raining, we'll have a nice bright day to explore."

"I like that idea even better!" Annie exclaimed, and apparently, so did the entire membership of the Hook and Needle Club. "Why don't we meet here after lunch and carpool?"

"If it's bright and sunny," Gwen added.

"Yes. If it's bright and sunny."

After the meeting, just as Annie was leaving A Stitch In Time, Kate called, "Wait up, Annie!"

The woman slipped on her denim jacket with crocheted epaulets as she hurried toward the front door. She gave Annie a nervous smile.

"Could we go to The Cup & Saucer for lunch?" she asked in an undertone. "I want to talk to you."

The request surprised Annie. "But don't you have to work?"

"Mary Beth is letting me have a long lunch today." She gave Annie a pleading look. "Please?"

Annie had planned to do research on the Harpers and Fairview, but a look into Kate's eyes changed her mind.

"Sure. I'm a little hungry."

Kate gave her a relieved smile. "Thanks! And lunch is my treat." Annie started to protest, knowing Kate didn't have a lot of extra money. "I mean it, Annie. I want to treat you."

"Well, then. I can't say no. Thank you."

Kate tucked her arm through Annie's and said as they went out the door, "Let's just walk. It's such a lovely day."

They sat near one of the windows at The Cup & Saucer where the midday sun flooded the world outside.

"I just love it here," Kate sighed after they ordered hamburgers and fries. "So homey and warm."

"It *is* nice," Annie agreed, sipping her tea. Since moving to Maine, she had learned more fully to enjoy hot tea as well as the preferred iced tea everyone drank in Texas.

"Oh, by the way, I have something for you." She reached in to her purse and withdrew the small card the red-haired woman had given her Saturday night at Sweet Nell's.

Kate took it and looked at the name. "Who is Nancy Crawford?"

"I don't know her, but she approached me the other night at Sweet Nell's—"

"You went to Sweet Nell's?! How was it? Did you sing? Did you have fun? I've been thinking about going out there."

Annie laughed.

"It was a lot of fun. And no, I did not sing, but Ian did."

Kate's eyes rounded. "Really? Our mayor got up in front of people and sang?"

"He's got a fantastic voice too."

Kate clapped her hands like a little girl. "I just think that's too cool!"

"It was fun," Annie said again. "But this is what I want to talk to you about." She tapped the card in Kate's hand. "The lady who gave me that card loved my shawl so much she wanted me to make her one—"

"Oh, Annie! You should!"

Annie shook her head. "I don't want to. But I thought you might. If you'd like to, you can borrow mine for the pattern. What's more, I think you might have a customer who'd buy a lot more creations from you."

"Really?" Kate looked down at the card. "That would be great. I'd love to sell more of my work." She glanced up. "Thank you, Annie! And you're sure you don't ... ?" She waved the card.

"Positive. I have other things to do, like the ongoing work at Grey Gables, and now, Fairview. My days are going to be full for a long time, I think."

"Well, thank you," Kate said again and tucked the card in her wallet. "I'll give the lady a call tomorrow." Then she took a deep breath, as though gathering her thoughts; she met Annie's eyes, and smiled.

"Annie," she said, pausing for a moment. Then she continued, "Annie, I want to tell you what happened to me."

That was a loaded statement. Kate had been through a lot in her life. What was it she now wanted to share? Even though Kate was older than LeeAnn, her wide-eyed view of the world often drew out Annie's nurturing instinct. Annie reached over and touched the woman's fine-boned hand.

"OK, honey. What do you want to tell me?"

Kate looked out the window for a moment, and then turned her gaze back to Annie.

"I saw my best friend after she died."

The words startled Annie, but she tried not to let it show. "Oh?"

Kate nodded. "I don't mean I saw her body in the casket.

I mean I saw *her*."

Annie gave little credence to the reported goings-on in the paranormal world so she said nothing, but merely waited for Kate to continue.

"Amanda and I were really good friends all through school. Then she got sick. And she got sicker and sicker, and she died." She said this all quickly, as if to get it out of the way. She looked out the window again, lost in her memories. "When she first got sick, I'd go over to her house and take her soup, or a casserole, or flowers, or a book. You know, something to let her know I was thinking of her."

She looked at Annie as though for approval, and Annie nodded again.

"I didn't know how sick she was. She didn't talk about it very much, other than to say she was tired, or feeling out of sorts. Flowers and food and good books to read weren't going to help her, but I didn't know that then. I noticed she got thinner, and her skin took on an odd pallor, and I realized something was seriously wrong. Amanda never told me she had cancer."

She took in another deep breath, staring down at the table top where she drew little circles with her fingertip.

"Then Vanessa was born, and she took up most of my time. The days slipped away. I didn't visit Amanda as often as I should have. When we talked on the phone, I usually cut it short. Babies need so much attention, and my husband started accusing me of neglecting him, so I felt like I had to give him more of my time, as well. Even though every day I thought about calling Amanda or visiting her, when Vanessa slept, I tried to rest. I was just exhausted, Annie. *Exhausted!*"

She inhaled, held her breath, and then let it out with painful slowness.

"Amanda died." She met Annie's gaze. "It had been more than two weeks since I'd spoken to my friend. She was gone, and I hadn't even told her how much I loved her. I figured she had thought I'd forgotten about her, or that I didn't care." Her eyes filled. "That was not true. I thought about her every day. But the hours and the minutes just slipped by until they became days. I never got to tell her goodbye."

Annie knew exactly what Kate felt. After all, she had done her own grandmother the same way, cutting back visits to Stony Point until visits were virtually nonexistent; then Gram died and there was no turning back the clock to recapture those missed days. Tears stung Annie's own eyes.

"Oh, Kate. I'm so sorry." She squeezed her friend's hand.

Kate nodded. "I knew you'd understand because you've mentioned a few times how hard it was on you when Betsy died—how you felt you'd let her down by not being there." She took a long drink, as though trying to wash down her wretchedness. "I dragged through the days after that, taking care of the baby and Harry, but not much else. I couldn't get it out of my head that I had been selfish and callous when my friend needed me so much."

"But, Kate, you had a new baby and a demanding husband to care for."

"Yes. And you had your own family down in Texas. A long way away."

They smiled sadly at each other for a bit, each one immersed in the painful memories.

"One day," Kate said in a voice so quiet that Annie had to

lean forward to hear her, "I was peeling potatoes for dinner, and someone knocked on my door. I opened the door," she stopped, swallowed hard and continued, "I opened the door, and Amanda stood there, all healthy and smiling. So very alive."

Annie gaped at her.

"I know, you think I'm crazy, don't you? But I swear it's true. I couldn't say a word. I just stared at her the way you're staring at me right now. Amanda tipped her head to one side, the way she would do sometimes, and said, 'Katie, you need to stop moping around like a wet dishrag and take care of yourself.' Then she kind of laughed and added, 'You are a great mom. I'm so proud of you, and so glad we grew up together. Take care of that baby.' Then she just fluttered her fingers in this little wave, turned around and walked away. She was gone before she reached the end of the sidewalk."

Annie didn't know what to say. The tale was both eerie and beautiful. Kate told it with such earnestness that Annie harbored no doubts something odd had occurred to her friend at some point. Maybe she had had a particularly vivid dream, tempered with loss and guilt.

"I was terrified," Kate said, looking purely miserable. "I had the chance to see my dear friend one last time, tell her goodbye, and instead I stood in that doorway like a frozen ninny, shaking from head to foot."

"Oh, Kate," Annie said. "You shouldn't feel badly about that. Seeing someone who has ... passed on—well, anyone would be frightened by that."

"But Amanda? Dear gentle Amanda? And she spoke to me so sweetly, with such comforting words. It's like I betrayed her twice."

Annie almost wished she had turned down this lunch invitation. What could she say that would both soothe and strengthen this young woman across from her?

"It's why I refused to be afraid at Fairview," Kate said while Annie still trolled for wisdom. "Fear had choked me once before, and I just was not going to let it happen again. I decided if I could help someone, anyone, under the same circumstances, I would."

"Well, then," Annie said, "you accomplished your goal. Without you, Peggy and Alice would still be screaming their heads off. Fairview would still be 'haunted,' and I would not be able to sell it. As they say back home 'Honey, you done good!'"

Kate searched her eyes eagerly, as if looking for deception.

"Truly, Kate," she continued. "You did me a huge favor. And I think you taught those two silly women who went along with us to buck up under ghostly pressures."

Kate's face broke into a smile.

"Thank you, Annie. I just knew you'd understand."

Annie could not fully comprehend or accept the whisper of the supernatural, but she understood Kate's turmoil.

Their lunch arrived, fragrant with the scent of dill pickles and grilled onions.

"You will keep my secret?" Kate said, pausing, as she reached for the ketchup, to fix an earnest gaze on her friend.

"Absolutely. Nary a peep from these lips."

"You're the best, Annie!"

~ 17 ~

Sunday afternoon, Annie transported half of the Hook and Needle Club members in her Malibu, and Jason, Stella's driver, drove the rest of them in her decade-old Lincoln Continental. Annie gazed somewhat enviously at that big old boat of a car and its roomy luxury, but she loved her Malibu and dreaded the day she would have to replace it. Wayne would never buy her another car, and the Malibu remained a treasure because it came from him.

Once they reached Fairview, the women in the Lincoln piled out, except Stella. She remained seated until Jason opened the door for her and offered his hand. She emerged as regally as a queen and clung to his hand a moment while she looked around.

"My goodness, Annie," she said, after a bit. "What have you gotten yourself into? And Jason, don't you dare let me slip and fall in that muddy yard. I may have on my old shoes and old clothes, but they are by no means muck boots and overalls."

In fact, Stella's shoes were sturdy but polished leather, and her slacks matched her jacket. Annie winced, thinking of the dust and dirt inside the house. Stella's lovely "old clothes" would look far less classy after an hour or two in the dust, grime, and cobwebs of Fairview.

"You want me to pick you up and carry you like a delicate princess?" Jason asked.

Her eyes flashed. "I do not! But if you let me fall, you'll be looking for another car to drive."

"Uh huh," he replied, with a wink at the other women. "Just step careful now."

The cottage looked even smaller once Jason and the entire membership of the Hook and Needle Club had gathered in the front room. The women whispered to each other as if they were in a funeral parlor.

"Well, ladies—and Jason—here it is! Three bedrooms, a couple of bathrooms, a kitchen and dining room. Not nearly as big as Grey Gables, but in need of as much renovation, I think! Shall I conduct a tour?"

"No reason to do that, Annie," Stella said. "We'll take our own tours."

And that is what they did, spreading out like crime-scene investigators, with as much pluck and confidence as Annie had ever seen on television.

"Well, Annie?"

She looked at Alice who had stayed in the living room with her.

"Well, Alice?"

"Where shall we look?"

"Do you really think we'll find anything?" Annie asked in an undertone. "I mean, really! Gram would never have kept anything of much importance here. Would she? The woman she rented it to was quite poor, and she used whatever was already here. I just don't think … . Oh, well, we're here now, so let's make the most of it."

Alice shrugged. "Look around again, Annie. Pictures

on the walls, beds made up, everything neat and tidy—just dirty from years of sitting here."

"I suppose you're right. Well, let's shuck the dust covers and see what we find."

Soon a cloud of dust hovered like a dreaded fog in every room. Depending upon the state of whatever found object was discovered, remarks of delight or dismay replaced the earlier hush.

"Annie, look at this!" or "Annie, come here!" seemed to be the call that came most often.

"We'll form a cleaning crew," Mary Beth announced at one point. She stood in the small hallway, fists on hips, shoulders squared in typical fashion. "We'll gather up cleaning supplies and polish this place up. Why, it's cute, once you can actually see it."

"It's darling," Stella said as she emerged from the back bedroom. "A perfect New England cottage. Why, once Wally has made the repairs you won't have a bit of trouble selling—or renting—this place!"

The back door opened with a creak of old hinges, just like every other door in Fairview. Jason's heavy steps crossed the kitchen floor, and he came into the hallway.

"Have you looked in the shed out back?"

"There's a shed out back?" Annie asked. She had not explored the grounds of the place at all.

Jason gave her a funny look. "Didn't you know that? Well, that's understandable, though. It's out behind that big cedar. It's not in nearly as good a shape as the house, but it's not bad. Look." He held up a couple of large, grimy tools with considerable rust on them. "This is a miter box," he said about the long wooden box with two open ends. "And this thing that looks a little like an iron is a hand plane to smooth or shave wood." He smiled broadly "These are just like the ones my grandfather used." His strong face softened with the memories; his eyes shone. "Grandpop's tools were sold off in an auction years ago, but I still remember watching him work with them. He built my mother a beautiful display cabinet, and the dining room set he and Grandma used. Built them out of maple."

"Wally would love to see those!" Peggy said.

Jason nodded. "I'm sure he would. It's just too bad that they've been left to rust." Annie looked at the man and said, "Take them, Jason, please."

He looked up, surprised. "Excuse me?"

"I want you to have those tools."

He looked down at the tools he held as though he had never seen them before, and then lifted his gaze to Annie again.

"Oh, no, Mrs. Dawson, I couldn't."

"Why not?"

"Because they're … they're old, and valuable, and … and you—"

"For goodness sake, Jason!" Stella fixed her familiar steely gaze on him. "Annie is offering them to you because she wants you to have them."

"Yes," Annie said quickly. "They've been in that toolshed ever so long, rusting away. Please, you take them and make use of them. Think of your grandfather when you work with them."

A smile began and then spread across his face.

"Thank you, ma'am," he said at last. "I … I'm not sure I will ever use them, but I'll surely clean them up and take care of them."

"Are there other tools out there, Jason?" Annie asked.

He nodded. "Yes, ma'am. There's a wood auger and a mortising chisel and some great old hammers. I even found some square nails. I bet all this stuff is left over from when this house was built."

"Take them too. If you don't, someone will surely steal them someday."

"I'm surprised someone hasn't already!" Gwen said stoutly.

"Wally says tools fetch a good price at flea markets and pawnshops."

Jason shot a look at Annie. She saw the expression and knew what he was about to say.

"I don't plan to haul a bunch of rusty old tools down to the pawnshop or sell them in a yard sale," she said firmly. "Jason, take them, if you want them. Share them with Wally Carson."

He grinned at her. "Yes, ma'am. I will. In fact, I'll just call Wally, and we'll divide them up between us."

"That's a fine idea. They're yours now, and you do with them as you please."

Everyone dispersed again, but about fifteen minutes later Stella came trotting out of the bedroom again, the soles of her shoes tapping against the old wood floor like woodpeckers.

"Annie, I found something!"

Annie turned from the stack of dusty books she was looking through, expecting to see a baby booty or a pot holder or yet another framed sampler. Instead she saw Stella waving a yellowed paper.

"I found this in an old cigar box in the bottom of a bottom drawer." A piece broke off and fell to the floor. "Oh! I must be careful. This is as brittle as thin glass. Look, Annie."

Reverently she handed over the paper. It was a newspaper article, fragile, dry, and crumbling.

Annie read the account aloud: "This reporter received word that the owner/builder of Fairview on Doss Road, David A. Ralston, died at his home in Buffalo, New York, last week. While Mr. Ralston was not well-known in our little community, our hearts go out to his loved ones."

There was no date on the clipping, but the discovery excited Annie.

"Well, that settles it then!" Annie said suddenly. "Thanks, Stella. I know what to do now. I don't know why I hadn't thought to do it before!"

~ 18 ~

The Hook and Needle Club members—and Jason—gently packed the old treasures they'd found in the Fairview cottage. Those treasures ranged from the tools Jason found, to a dust-coated oil painting, samplers and quilts.

"Please take anything you want," Annie told her friends. "I have more than enough at Grey Gables. And the less that is in Fairview the easier it will be to clean the place."

"Well, I was sort of hoping we'd have an encounter with the paranormal," Gwen said, laughing, as they stood in the front yard before leaving.

"Oh, no!" said Alice. "If by paranormal you mean scampering rodents, I'm just as glad not to have seen any. Of course, on a warm sunny day like this, I suppose they are more apt to stay hidden."

"Gwen," Annie said, "if I get even a hint of a ghost out here, I will definitely call on you to join our team."

As soon as she was home, showered and in clean clothes, Annie settled down on the sofa with her laptop. She was so tired she ached, but she knew she would be unable to relax until she had at least started her search for anything about David Ralston now that she had a tidbit to get her started.

She had never been a great one for using the computer, except as needed for business at the car dealership. Listening to younger people chatter about Google and Facebook and Twitter and all the rest of it left her feeling old and left out. She reasoned that with so much going on in her life, really, who needed the complications of the technological age creating more chaos? She bought this laptop, planning to use it to keep up with LeeAnn, Herb and the kids, but she much preferred the telephone or even an old-fashioned letter. For a long time, her research forays had been accomplished at the Stony Point library, but she finally had taken the step to bring Grey Gables into cyberspace. She had recently added an Internet connection and a wireless modem. She knew LeeAnn would be proud.

"Now, Miss Annie," she said, flexing her fingers above the keyboard as if she were about to play a concerto, "*you* are moving into the modern age."

When the Internet was up, she typed in "David Ralston Buffalo New York." Several links came up that led her to contemporary men by that name. But she finally found what she was looking for: an obituary from 1950. It was rather lengthy, and included a grainy photograph that gave little indication as to the man's looks.

"David Alan Ralston, 62, of Buffalo, New York, died in his home, November 3, 1950. The son of Bert and Ingrid Bale Ralston, Mr. Ralston was born December 12, 1887, in Cleveland, Ohio. He owned the DaRal sporting-goods chain until 1945. He was preceded in death by his parents and a brother, Henry Ralston. Mr. Ralston is survived by his niece, Elizabeth A. Ralston."

Annie looked again at the name of the one relative: Elizabeth A. Ralston.

She typed in the name. A slew of links filled the page.

She clicked one at random.

"Elizabeth Alta Ralston, daughter of Henry Bledsoe Ralston and Emma Louise Fraley Ralston, graduated with honors from Miami University in Oxford, Ohio, June 8, 1940."

"Alta!"

She read no farther, but closed the link, and as fast her fingers could move across the keyboard, she tapped out Elizabeth Alta Ralston Harper into the empty bar at the top of the screen.

Pay dirt!

It looked like a small, inconsequential news item scanned from an old Weston, Ohio, newspaper and published in 1943.

"Joseph Elmer Harper and Elizabeth Ralston were quietly married June 26 in a small ceremony held at the home of the groom's parents in Weston. Mr. Harper, a 1935 graduate of Weston-Bailey High School is employed at the Daniels Meat Packing Plant. They will make their home in the McKinley Heights Apartments on Sherman Avenue."

Annie clicked on other links, finding more newspaper items, watching as the columns grew longer and the accounts more detailed, until her head buzzed with all of the information. And never, in all the pages she had scrolled through, did she find so much as a single, simple mention of Stony Point, Maine. If she could just find where the couple now lived … .

Then she found an obituary, and her heart sank. It was not a single obit, but a double one. The Harpers had died on the same day and were buried side by side in a cemetery in Ohio. As carefully as she read David Ralston's obituary, she studied this one about the Harpers.

"J.E. was preceded in death by his parents, Elmer and Mamie Harper, and Elizabeth A. Harper was preceded in death by her parents, Henry and Emma Louise Ralston, and an uncle David Ralston of Buffalo, N.Y. Survivors include sons Bruce Calvin Harper and wife Melissa of Weston, Kevin Daniel Harper and wife Natalie of Cleveland, Ohio, and one granddaughter, Trudy Harper Jenkins of Richmond, Ind. The Harpers have a host of friends and neighbors who mourn their passing. Interment will be at Weston Hills Cemetery."

Annie looked up from the screen and squeezed shut her eyes. They felt thick and dull. Her neck ached. How long had she been at this online research anyway? She looked around. The room was dark except for the eerie glow of her laptop, and she had not even noticed it until right then. A glance out the front room window proved the day had advanced well past twilight. She really should finish the search tomorrow and get some rest.

But she refused. She had come this far, and quitting held not one iota of appeal. Even with a stiff neck, dull eyes, raging headache, and empty stomach she persevered.

She typed in Bruce Calvin Harper. And found his obituary.

Kevin Daniel Harper. Obituary.

Annie got a sick feeling in the pit of her belly.

"One more try," she whispered and tapped keys to spell, "Trudy Harper Jenkins."

She pressed enter.

The screen offered a link with the woman's name. She

clicked the URL and found the website for a small private school. Trudy Harper Jenkins was alive and well, teaching fourth grade school in Sidney, Ohio.

Annie scanned the screen, found the phone number for the school and reached for her cell phone. At some point, Boots had silently entered the room and now sat on the arm of the sofa, blinking at her.

"How long have you been there?" Annie asked the cat. She held her cell phone, stared at it a moment, and then muttered to herself and Boots, "What grammar school would be in session at this time of night and on a Sunday, anyway?"

She started to put the phone down, but then changed her mind. She dialed information. A short time later she had the home phone number for the woman who seemed to be the only link between Fairview, the Harpers, and Annie's own dear grandmother.

~ 19 ~

nnie listened as the phone rang several times. Just when she about decided to cut the connection, she heard a click. She perked up, ready to greet the person on the other end.

"Hello. You have reached the phone of Sam and Trudy Jenkins. Please leave your name and phone number, and we will return your call as soon as we can. Thank you."

The beep to signal voice mail caught Annie off-guard, though she was not sure why it should. Everyone had voice mail or an answering machine these days. In fact, she reached more answering services than she did real people, but was never prepared.

"Umm. Hello. My name is Annie Dawson, and I'm from Stony Point, Maine. I am looking for information about a couple named Joseph and Alta Harper who lived here in the 1980s. Um, I'd like to talk to you, if you're willing. There is a ... well, I'd rather just talk to you instead of leaving a message." She paused, and nearly cut the connection when she remembered to give her phone number. "Thank you!" she added hurriedly, before she was cut off.

Upstairs she changed into her pajamas, brushed her teeth and hair, and paused long enough to look for fresh gray strands. She fluffed her hair with her fingers, arranging, and smoothing.

"Time for a touch up and a trim," she muttered, narrowing her eyes critically at the reflection. Then she met her own gaze and said, "And time to stop talking to yourself!"

At last, Annie crawled between the fresh, smooth sheets she had put on the bed that morning. She snuggled down with the covers cuddling her. She was tired, but didn't expect sleep to come easily. Her mind was too full of discovery.

Boots, who usually slept on her own little cushion, leaped onto the bed and padded gently up to Annie's face. Her tiny nose twitched softly as she drew closer. One small lick with her rough tongue, right on the end of Annie's nose, another sniff or two along the human cheek and ear, and then Boots gave a silent meow and backtracked a few steps. She kneaded the covers a few times, and then curled comfortably in a ball, nestled against Annie's chest. The thrumming purr of the cat's contented presence vibrated against Annie's body and calmed her as soothingly as a lullaby.

Annie drifted, her tired body relaxing into another state of being.

Ah, yes, she thought, floating. *Beautiful, glorious sleep....*

The tone of her cell phone seemed ten times louder and more shrill than necessary, yanking her with suddenness out of that bliss. Annie gasped and sat up, lost for a moment.

Her first thought raced to LeeAnn. Something dire must have happened for her daughter to call this late at night. But a glance at the bedside clock proved only a few minutes had passed since she had gone to bed. It was not even ten o'clock yet. She fumbled with the cell phone for a second or two.

"Hello," she croaked. She cleared her throat and spoke again. "Hello?"

"Hello. This is Trudy Jenkins. I'm returning your call."

Annie sat straight up in bed, wide awake in an instant. Boots yowled in protest and jumped to the floor.

"Yes!" she said. "I mean, thank you for calling."

"You said you knew my grandparents?" The tone was cautious, perhaps a bit hopeful.

"No, actually. I didn't know them, but my grandmother did."

There was a long pause.

"In Maine?"

"Yes. Stony Point."

"My goodness." This came faintly, as if the caller had suddenly reeled from the mouthpiece. "My goodness. Ms. Dawson, you don't know … . We've wondered … . I mean, it's been more than twenty-five years, and my family all thought Grandpa and Grandma … . I need to sit down."

Annie hardly knew what to think. Was the woman on the other end of the conversation as flummoxed as she sounded? Why was she at a loss for words? Had Annie fumbled her message that much?

"Are you all right?" she asked. She turned on the bedside lamp, as if the light could help her see Trudy Jenkins.

"Yes. I'm fine." She sounded stronger, more in control. "Excuse me, just one moment." Annie heard sounds of papers and shuffling; then Trudy Jenkins said, "I'm sorry. I just had to sit down." She laughed. "And get something to write on. Your message so stunned me that I didn't even stop to think before I returned your call. I apologize. I was gone …

open house at the school tonight. Oh, my."

"I understand. I'm sure my message was a little garbled in content. You know how you never expect to go to voice mail but almost always do."

"Yes. And you're never prepared!"

"Exactly."

They laughed together, and then Annie said, "I am so glad to finally make contact with someone who had some connection with Joe and Alta Harper."

"Mrs. Dawson, you have no idea how long I've waited to hear from you."

Annie blinked. "From me?"

"Well, not you in particular. That is, I've waited to hear from someone, anyone, who might have known my grandparents the year they disappeared."

~ 20 ~

"*Disappeared*? They disappeared?"

"Yes. But you knew that. Didn't you?"

This time it was Annie's turn to pause. An old abandoned house, and now a disappearance? What next?

"I'm sorry," she said. "I didn't know that. Were they ever found?"

"Oh yes. Yes, of course! But ... how could you not know that?" Trudy's voice was tense, the words curt and clipped.

Annie felt affronted, but Trudy immediately gasped out, "I'm so sorry! Please forgive me for snapping like that. It's just that hearing from you has just taken me so by surprise, even though I've waited all these years."

"It's all right. Don't feel badly. But why don't we take events one at a time? I'll tell you what little I know, and you can fill me in on what you know. Then perhaps knowing all that, we'll be able to solve both our mysteries!"

"I like that idea. Yes. Please tell me as much as you can."

Annie scrunched up her pillow, piled another one top of it, settled comfortably against them and said, "I'd be glad to."

She explained about Gram and the attic and all the treasurers she had found up there since she had lived at Grey Gables. She told about the huge box of yarn and how her search for a place to store it led her to discovering the deed.

"I'd never heard of Fairview, and certainly Gram never

said a single word about owning another property. But the mystery got so deep when no one in Stony Point could remember your grandparents. In fact, no one had even heard of them."

"I see! Well, I certainly understand how that could rouse intrigue and curiosity." Trudy chuckled. "I'm not sure I'd have the patience to chase down details, but I'm so glad you did!"

"Believe me, this has not been easy. I have basically run into dead end after dead end, until now."

"I'm sure that has been extremely frustrating for you."

"It has!" Annie agreed. "Almost maddening, in fact."

"No doubt. But you persevered and found me!"

Annie smiled. "Yes! So, Trudy, did you know my grandmother?"

"No, I'm sorry to say that until this moment, I only knew her through what my grandfather told us. And it was a long time before he spoke of her at all. For a while, all anyone in my family knew was that we woke up one day and my grandparents were gone. They had simply vanished, and we couldn't find them. The note Grandpa had left was cryptic and short, and all efforts to find him and Grandma were fruitless."

"So they came to Stony Point, but no one knew?"

"One day about a year or so later, they returned. Just as suddenly and with just as much mystery as they had left. We never knew what had happened that year until a couple of days before they died. No matter how often we asked, they both would just give us these sweet little smiles and say nothing. But then Grandma became very ill. She pretty much lost touch with the world around her and went down-hill fast. Grandpa was healthy, but her deterioration was hard on him. They loved each other so much. Then one day … . Well, I guess he sensed the end was near. He just started talking. And he told us about that year."

~ 24 ~

June 1986: Joe glanced across the front seat as Alta reached up to adjust the sun visor on her side of the car. She had napped off and on for the last hundred or so miles, but now the sun's bright new rays shot straight through the windshield and pierced their eyes. No amount of change to the visor would shield her eyes at this early hour. He flipped down the pair of clip-ons he had attached to his driving glasses before they left home. The cool rays of the tinted glass eased his vision.

"You Okay, honey?" he asked.

She yawned and stretched her legs in as much space as the small rental car allowed, and then fished in her purse.

"I'm fine," she said as she withdrew a pair of large dark-framed sunglasses from her purse and settled them on her small nose. She turned her head to face him. "How 'bout you, Joey?"

He smiled at the sweet old name she called him, stretched out his right arm and grabbed her hand.

"I could do with a break pretty soon. Maybe we'll stop for breakfast in the next town. What do you say to that?"

He lifted her hand to his lips and kissed her thin fingers. The diamonds from her wedding band caught the sunlight and shared it with the rest of the world. They would never see the rest of her jewelry shine that way again.

"I'd like breakfast, I think. I've been too nervous to eat very much these last few days."

"I know, honey. I know."

Hand in hand, they rode in silence as the miles stretched behind and before, full of regret and hope, threat and promise.

Just like our lives, Joe thought.

The sun inched upward, and the car's interior warmed. He refrained from turning on the air conditioner. Along with sleepless nights and loss of appetite, Alta had taken to being cold a lot lately. When they got to Stony Point, he was going to insist she see a doctor, just to make sure she was all right. He figured the pressure of these last months had done this, but stress could be a killer. He never took chances with his darling's health.

"'Grandma's Rocking Chair Cookies','" she read as they passed a huge billboard. "Do you suppose Grandma makes them in a rocking chair?"

He chuckled at her attempted humor, squeezed her fingers. It meant she hadn't given up completely.

"Maybe you're supposed to eat them in a rocking chair," he said.

"I like that idea better."

"Maybe they'll have Grandma's Rocking Chair Cookies in Maine."

"Maybe."

"If they don't, you'll have to bake us some."

She nodded.

"Maybe we can sit on the porch and eat cookies. Or on the beach at night, next to a big old bonfire."

He wanted things to be as normal as possible, and normal

included Alta smiling and feeling lighthearted. She said nothing; her silence scared him.

"Remember that time, where was it? Costa Rica, or Cancún, maybe, where we took that long moonlit walk and there were those college kids around a bonfire? Remember? They invited us to eat hotdogs and marshmallows, and told us all about their grandparents. They called us Mema and Pepa. Remember? They were good kids to treat us geezers like youngsters."

Her smile was a mere shade of its normal brilliance.

"Yes. That was sweet of them."

Silence for a while, then …

"Joe? Joe, are we doing the right thing? Just leaving this way?"

He tried not to sigh audibly.

"Sweetheart, we've been over this more times than I can count."

"I know. But I can't help but feel there was something else—something more we could have done, somehow."

"No. There was nothing else we could have done. I couldn't face Bruce or Kevin, not after everything that happened. You know that."

She lifted the sunglasses long enough to wipe tears with a tissue.

"I know. Oh, honey, I know! But it's just so hard to leave them, not saying goodbye, not kissing Trudy, or hugging our kids. Joe. Joe, I just don't think I can …."

Her sobs broke his heart. Alta, who had believed in him when he had had nothing to offer but love and promises, had given him her youth and her heart and two beautiful sons.

But now all that was behind them, back there in a world they would never see again. Look what she had: A few suitcases. Her cross-stitch. And him.

It wasn't easy, that trip to coastal Maine. They were not young anymore, and their joints stiffened after sitting so long in the small car. By the time they passed Stony Point and pulled into the driveway at Fairview, the day was far advanced, and a chill had settled into everything. They had stopped at a fast-food place in some little town an hour or so ago, and the greasy food had settled uncomfortably in his system. In fact, he felt a little queasy. Joe pulled out the suitcase that held their night clothes and linens, and he left everything else in the car until he could unload tomorrow.

"Fairview," he muttered as he trudged behind Alta toward the cottage door. He dreaded to see what was inside the old house Alta's uncle had left to her. No one had set foot in the place in years.

She unlocked the door and opened it, stepping aside for him to pass through with his burden.

"Get the lights, will you, honey?" he said.

"We have electricity?"

"I called the utility companies days ago and sent them a money order. We'd better have lights—and heat and water."

Alta fumbled, feeling along the wall in the semidarkness, clicked the switch and threw the room into bright relief. Joe looked around. Dull with dust, the room still presented a homey ambiance.

"We'll get someone in here to clean tomorrow," Alta said with her customary optimism. "It will be beautiful. I'll buy some new curtains. Those are ancient. Some new furniture."

"Honey."

She looked at him, her eyes dim with fatigue in spite of her cheerful demeanor and confident words.

"Let's go to bed now, and talk about this place tomorrow."

A good night's sleep on a bed Alta hastily and clumsily made up with fresh linens, gave them new energy. But they did not hire help to clean. They did it themselves. For Alta, it was the first time in many years she had tackled such chores. And the new furnishings and draperies she wanted? That would never happen. They had to make do with what was in the cottage.

Life in Maine proved more difficult than either one anticipated. Torn from everything familiar, they felt thrust into what seemed to be nothing more than a backwoods cabin far from the privileged lifestyle they had lived for so many years. Alta wanted to mingle with the locals, and longed for a social life, but Joe protested.

"You know we have people looking for us right now, honey. It's best if we stay here, out of sight as much as possible. It'll get better by and by, I promise."

"But people in town think our names are Jim and Barb Johnson. They won't link us with HarperTown Investments. No one will know."

"I'd rather be safe than sorry. Maybe in a few years. After the scandal dies, after everyone knows the truth, maybe then we'll try to become a part of Stony Point society. But for now, honey, our social circle has to be just you and me, and the two channels we can get on TV."

She gave him a sweet smile and agreed, but the loneliness on her face haunted his dreams every night. The worst part, of course, was leaving behind their sons and their granddaughter. He told himself that, for a time, Kevin and Bruce would likely bear the brunt of Joe's retreat from the situation, but nothing like they would have had to endure if he had stayed for the media circus and finger-pointing. At least his family would be safe, and that was the most important part of all of it to Joe. Investigators would uncover the truth behind the corruption, and everyone would know he had been used as a pawn in his own undoing. His family would not have to watch the airing of dirty laundry Joe had not soiled.

The only illegal thing Joe Harper had ever done in his life was to buy a new identity for himself and his beloved wife, and no one would ever know about that if he could help it.

One evening in late autumn, she sat near the fireplace, working on a large cross-stitch. She stopped working and stared glumly into the fire. Joe turned from the television and watched her for a moment. She never moved, and he knew she was lost in yesterday again.

"Honey?" he said quietly.

"I've run out of the dark blue," she said, not moving so much as an eyelash.

"What? You mean blue thread?"

"I'm out of it, and I can't finish my piece."

Finally she looked across the room at him. Firelight played across her features and for the first time he noticed how she had aged. The shadows deepened the wrinkles around her mouth and eyes. Her hair, always a chic, short light brown hung loose around her face and showed its true gray. These days, there was no money for her weekly trip to the stylist. In fact, the cash they had brought with them was the emergency stash out of the safe at home, and it dwindled at an alarming rate, even with his careful eye on it.

Joe tried with no success to find a job. No one wanted to hire a man in his late sixties, especially a man who could not prove a work history. Alta was too frail these days for work that was more than household chores and simple cooking. He gazed at her now, sweet and delicate, the love of his life.

Elizabeth Alta Ralston, daughter of one of Ohio's leading families, virtually cut herself off from that family to marry Joe, the penniless dreamer. Together, with hard work, determination and faith in each other, they had come up from the depths to achieve material gain beyond anything Joe had ever imagined.

All that had been taken away from them in a matter of a few days, and now … now he was too old to recover what they had lost. His spirit was broken, his faith shattered. But a look at his wife's face was enough to give him pause. She had given up everything for him. Everything. Surely, there was something he could do.

"Tomorrow," he said, "let's go into town to the little craft shop. What's it called—It's Time to Stitch? You can buy some more blue thread."

Her face lit up, her smile trembling.

"It's called A Stitch in Time. But can we afford it, Joe?"

"We'll afford it," he said stoutly. Even if he had to sell his blood, his darling would have that dark blue thread.

The next day, Alta roamed A Stitch in Time, her face

glowing and as relaxed as he had seen since they left their home in Ohio. Joe stood well back from customers and staff, his cap pulled low over his brow, though he knew no one would know him, especially in Maine after all this time.

Alta stood next to an elderly woman who studied the stock of embroidery floss with the same intense reverence as Alta. Joe smiled, watching the women pick up thread, touch it, hold it out to the light, put it aside and look at another.

The elderly woman spoke, smiling, and looked at Alta. For a moment, Joe's wife simply regarded the friendly lady beside her with bright eyes, and then she replied. Within moments, the two were engaged in deep conversation, animated gestures, wide smiles, and a laugh or two. Together they looked at pattern books, exclaiming over whatever they found in them.

After a bit, Alta turned, looked at her husband, and then beckoned the woman to come with her. They approached where he still stood, out of the way, near the entrance.

"J-Jim, may I present Betsy Holden. Mrs. Holden, my husband, Jim—" A brief look of panic washed across her face, as if she had lost something, then she blurted, "Johnson! Jim Johnson."

Betsy Holden was a compact, neat-as-a-pin woman, her snowy hair perfectly styled and simple. Her smile was warm and friendly but not saccharin or fawning. She met his eyes squarely, her handshake firm. He liked the woman immediately, and from the shining expression on Alta's face, he knew she had found a friend. He just hoped Betsy presented no problems to their anonymity.

Over the next several weeks, the trio's friendship blossomed, but Joe cautioned Alta against revealing their true identity to a woman who was such a moving force and minor celebrity in the small town.

"Not that I don't trust Betsy," he said. "She's become a good friend, and I'm glad we met her, but you know as well as I do that sometimes things just slip out in conversation. If she doesn't know anything, she can't reveal anything."

Alta agreed. Although it was easy for him to see how much she yearned to spill all her fears to someone, she guarded their secret well.

That winter, their money ran out. Alta's diamond-encrusted wedding band waited redemption in the pawnshop, and the few hundred dollars it brought them would not last long. A child of the Great Depression, Joe knew how to survive the rough times. The fireplace became the main source of heat once the oil ran out. Wood, at least, was plentiful. They brought their bed into the front room, tacked quilts and blankets over every doorway and lived in that one room. The old car they'd bought when they first moved to Stony Point stayed in the driveway except for rare trips into town.

Rice. Ramen noodles. Beans. This became their diet, and who knew how long that would last? Joe often fished from the pier, and he caught mackerel, but he knew they needed more. He had to do something.

The next day, he sat on the sofa of Grey Gables and watched Betsy Holden pour tea in a pretty blue patterned cup.

"How's Barb?" she asked. He still felt odd when anyone called Alta that name. Maybe if they had called each other Jim and Barb at home, the names would have become more familiar, easier to use, easier to hear. "She looked a little pale the last time I saw her," Betsy continued. She handed him the cup. As he took it, Betsy's eyes met his. "In fact, she doesn't look well at all."

He nodded, sipped the tea too quickly and burned his lips.

"I know. Things aren't … good for us."

She settled back in her chair, ankles crossed neatly, gray skirt lying in smooth folds. Her red cardigan had a single, tiny cross-stitched snowbird. Alta had done that, and the fact that an artisan such as Betsy would wear his wife's simple design filled him with pride.

"And they have not been good for a while, I suspect," she said, blowing gently across the top of her tea.

"That's true. That's so true." He blinked back tears and swallowed down rising shame.

"Do you want to talk about it?"

He gulped another drink, let it scald his tongue and throat, hoping the pain would sideswipe his humiliation.

"Betsy." His voice had lost the authoritative timbre gleaned from years of being the controlling force of HarperTown. He couldn't meet her gaze for a moment, but when he finally did, he saw her eyes were filled with compassion and patience.

"I need a job," he whispered. "I need work … badly."

She set her cup on the small piecrust table next to her. "Just how bad are things, Jim?"

He took a deep breath. "We're broke. Completely broke."

"Social Security doesn't stretch far," she said.

He did not tell her they received no checks from the government. How could they? Jim and Barb Johnson had no previous life in which either had made any contributions to the system.

"I assume you've looked for work in town?"

He nodded. "No one wants to hire an oldster like me. Not that they said it in so many words. That would be against the law. But I know."

"You never have told me what kind of work you can do, Jim."

He shrugged. "I'm willing to do anything."

Betsy gave him a sharp look, and he knew his evasive reply was not what she wanted to hear.

"Well, I do have a number of things you could help with around here," she said after a bit, looking around. "Of course, many of them will have to wait until the end of winter. Would you be willing to wait until warm weather to do the work?"

His heart dropped. Waiting another three or four months? How could they survive?

We'll just have to. That's all. We'll have to.

"I'll be happy to do whatever work you want done, Betsy."

She smiled and rose from her chair. "No, no. Stay seated. I'll be back." When she returned a minute later, she held out a check to him. "Do me a favor, and take this as a deposit on the work you're going to do. You see, if I pay you now, you can't change your mind later." She smiled broadly as he took the check. "There will be more as the season progresses. Get your muscles toned up, Jim. You're going to need them!"

Betsy's generous check saw them comfortably through the winter, and that spring, those years of hard physical labor as a young man flooded back to Jim. By mid-May he felt stronger and more vigorous than he had at the age of forty. None of that sitting behind the desk for him these days. Gardening, digging, weeding, planting. Repairing the porch floor, smoothing the rain damage from the driveway. Cutting grass with a power mower, not a rider.

On Memorial Day, Betsy had dinner with them. The simple, traditional fare of grilled burgers, potato salad and chocolate cake suited them all, but when she started to clear the table, Alta unexpectedly burst into tears.

"Honey, what's wrong?" Joe said, rushing to her side.

She buried her face in her hands and sobbed. Joe and Betsy exchanged a look. Betsy stood on Alta's other side and gently rubbed her back in small circles.

"Let her cry," she murmured to Joe. "Just for a bit. Then she'll be ready to talk."

So they waited, Betsy with placid patience, Joe with his heart breaking to see his wife hurting. Alta finally raised her face, red and damp, looking as lost as Joe had ever seen her.

"I miss my family!" she blurted. "I want to see my sons. I want to hug Trudy. I want to go home!"

Joe had known Alta's homesickness never fully abated, but he had been so busy these last few weeks rebuilding his pride that he had really given little thought to how alone she must feel with him away so often. She went with him to Betsy's from time to time, but Betsy was a busy woman and Alta refused to encroach on her time. Joe had deluded himself, obviously, by believing she was settling in to this new world, growing used to such a drastic change in her life.

Guilt engulfed him as he stared helplessly at his wife.

"Then, my dear, you should go home," Betsy said reasonably.

Alta's sobs hushed instantly. She and Joe stared at the other woman.

"Why do you put yourself through this pain?" Betsy continued. "If you miss your home and your children, why are you *here*?"

The silence that hung over them was so thick Joe thought he could grasp it with his fingers.

"We … uh … we can't go home," he said quietly to Betsy.

She met his eyes straight on. "Why not?"

Silence hovered again, thickened with tension and need.

"Tell her, Joe," Alta whispered. "*Tell her!*"

He looked at his wife's red-rimmed eyes, her grief-ravished face, the pallor of her skin. With the violent suddenness of a summer thunderstorm, the knowledge of what his decision had done to her reverberated through every cell of his body.

"*Tell her!*"

And so he did. Leaving out names and places, he explained how he had built an investment business from the ground up, how he and Alta had raised two children in the home of their dreams, how life had been so good for them. He told her how he had listened to his partner, an old and trusted friend, enthuse over the vast possibilities of a lakeside luxury development being created by an up-and-coming real estate company. The partner vowed he would offer his mother's eyeteeth to invest if he had to. And Joe listened to the man. Listened with such faith and confidence that he neglected to research the company or thoroughly go through their prospectus himself. Instead, he invested far too much capital and far too much faith—perhaps he had just grown old and gullible like a senior citizen falling for a high-pressure sales pitch over the telephone. He found out too late that the lake-front property was protected land, a wildlife refuge.

It was collusion on his partner's part—out-and-out fraud, but the damage had been done. Their faces were on TV and in the newspapers. There were late-night phone calls and threats. It had been more than good-hearted, trusting Joe Harper could take. In their attorney's office, Joe and Alta quickly signed papers to sell everything they owned in an attempt to repair the damage, but it was too late.

"Crooked schemers," he said. "They tore it all limb from limb, destroyed everything and left my investors with nothing. My sons, my home, my friends—everything ruined."

Betsy listened to every word, intently, her heart clearly in her expression. But now she leaned back in her chair and regarded him dispassionately.

"Running away was probably not your best option," she said. He nodded miserably. "Why *are* you here, Jim?" She obviously had missed Alta's use of his real name. "Why come all this way?"

"We had to get away," Alta told her. "I owned Fairview. My uncle willed it to me years ago, and Stony Point is a long way from Weston, Ohio. We knew if we weren't around, the media would find a new story and leave our family alone."

"And did they?"

Joe bent his head, more ashamed than any time in his life. He felt like a wretched, self-serving coward.

"The truth came out shortly after we left home. I kept up with the story, and when it was buried on a back page, I knew it was over. My partner will go to prison, and our family has been cleared of all wrong doing. But our sons lost everything."

"Including their mother and father."

Joe felt like his insides were being ripped out.

"Jim," Betsy said, "you have to go back. You know that, don't you? Stony Point, Maine, is no place for you and Barb."

He looked at Alta. He knew she would not last another year in Fairview. He knew they had to go back and face whatever music played for them upon their return.

"Jim?"

He looked up and into Betsy's kind, warm eyes.

"Yes. We'll go back."

～ 22 ～

"Grandpa said he was very careful not to tell Betsy or anyone in Stony Point their real names or where they came from," Trudy told Annie that night on the phone. "He didn't want any of us to be hurt any more than necessary. He asked Betsy to promise never to try to find them once they left and never to talk about them to anyone."

"Well, she certainly kept that promise." Annie replied with considerable feeling. "I've found no one in the town who had ever heard of them. I suppose changing their names had something to do with that, but Gram was great about honoring the wishes of others."

Trudy gave a soft little sigh. "She must have been a wonderful woman. I wish I had met her."

"She was terrific."

"After Grandma and Grandpa passed away, Dad and Uncle Bruce talked about getting in touch with Betsy to thank her for all she had done, but they realized Grandpa's wishes were to keep that part of his life out of the light. Coming back to Ohio, living a simple life in a small house was a far cry from the mansion they'd left in Weston. But they adapted to it well. In fact, all of us did. We went from 'riches to rags,' and while it wasn't easy, it certainly wasn't as awful as it could have been if they'd never returned."

"I believe I read an obituary for your father."

"Yes. Dad and Mom were killed in a boating accident in 1997, and Uncle Bruce died of kidney failure in 1999."

"I'm so sorry. It's so hard to lose loved ones." She thought of Wayne and felt the familiar stab in her heart.

"Yes, so hard. But I have a wonderful husband and twin girls. Zoë and Beth. They're twelve."

The women chatted briefly about their families, compared notes regarding twins, and then Annie brought the conversation back to Fairview.

"I've been trying to find out why my grandmother has ownership of Fairview. Did you know why your grandparents signed it over to her?"

"Grandpa said when they left Stony Point, they stopped at Grey Gables and gave Betsy the key to Fairview. They asked her to check on it in a month or so, just make sure things were okay. But Grandpa, always clever, had registered the deed in her name, and left it on the dining table for her to find. He left a note with it saying that giving her Fairview was their way of thanking her for getting them back on their feet and opening their eyes. He asked her to destroy the note and never tell anyone she met them. Until that moment, I'm sure Betsy never knew their real names."

Annie sat on her bed and stared into the darkness of the bedroom beyond the reach of her nightstand lamp. There was so much to assimilate after these many weeks of dead ends.

"Have you ever been to Stony Point?" she asked Trudy.

"No. But I would love to come someday, and see Grey Gables and Fairview. And A Stitch in Time—if it's still there. Grandma loved it so much."

Annie smiled. "It's still here and going strong."

"Then if I ever get to Maine, I surely want to see that wonderful shop."

* * *

Late afternoon shadows slanted across the land around Grey Gables. Annie stood a moment on the edge of her front porch, looking toward the road with anticipation.

A hearty chowder simmered on the stove. The house was clean, well-lit, and two spare rooms lay in readiness. Trudy Jenkins, her husband, and twin girls would arrive in time for dinner, if all went according to plan. During the last couple of months, Annie and Trudy had become friends through Facebook, e-mail and phone calls. It had not taken much persuasion from Annie to talk Trudy into visiting Stony Point.

The members of the Hook and Needle Club, Jason, Ian, and Wally had all pitched in and spruced up Fairview until the cottage fairly glowed. Tomorrow, Annie would take the Jenkins to the property that had once belonged to them— and would again very soon. The deed lay on the shining walnut table in Fairview's small dining room, signed by Annie. It now registered full ownership to Trudy Harper Jenkins.

Annie smiled a little, thinking of the moment she would return the property to its rightful owner.

She sighed happily, turned and went back into the front room. The Jenkins family would be there soon, but until then, she could work on her current project.

Annie picked up the deep green, oversized afghan she

was making for LeeAnn. For a moment, she examined the intricate Queen Anne's Lace stitches lovingly worked out of the yarn LeeAnn had sent her. She settled down in the armchair near the window so she could see the road.

With great contentment and much happiness, Annie looped the green yarn comfortably through her fingers and crocheted the next row. When she looked up again, she saw headlights coming up her driveway.

She rose and went to the door, a welcome-home invitation on her lips, warming her heart.

About The Author

K.D. McCrite grew up on a dairy farm in southern Missouri. She taught herself to crochet when she was ten years old and has been in love with it ever since. She graduated from Drury University with a degree in psychology. An avid reader who longed to tell stories that entertained and enthralled readers, K.D. has written since the age of twelve. Besides three previously published novels, her work has appeared in regional and national publications. K.D. lives in the Arkansas Ozarks with her husband, four dogs and one cat.

*J*oin Annie Dawson and the members of the Hook and Needle Club of Stony Point, Maine, as they track down mysteries connected with the contents found in the attic of Annie's ancestral home, Grey Gables. There will be danger, adventures and heartwarming discoveries in the secrets Annie unearths—secrets about her own family as well as the townspeople of this charming seacoast town in central Maine. Let the good people of Stony Point warm your heart and the mysteries of Annie's Attic keep you on the edge of your seat.